Married To the Game

Married To The Game

Chunichi

www.urbanbooks.net

Married to the Game

Urban Books
74 Andrews Ave.
Wheatley Heights, NY 11798

©copyright 2005 Chunichi

ISBN 0-9747025-9-5
First Printing December 2005
Printed in the United States of America

10 9 8 7 6 5 4 3

This book is dedicated to

all those who have made a positive impact on my life.

ACKNOWLEDGMENTS

As you may expect, first I would like to thank God for bringing me this far. I never thought I would be in such a place, and to be honest, at times I was ready to give up. As with any blessing, the Devil recognizes it and tries to still our happiness. Indeed he tried, but God picked me up and carried me through the storm. And now that the storm is over, the sun is shining brighter than I have ever seen before. Thank you, God, for such a wonderful gift!

To all my fans, thank you more than anything. Without you all, there is no me. I never understood the impact of my writing until I began to interact with my readers. The emails, reviews, shout-outs and book signings keep me motivated to write more and more each day.

To my literary family, thank you. Carl Weber and Roy Glenn with Urban Books, thank you for your patience. If I didn't finish this book, I don't know who would choke me first, you all or my fans. But I did it. We all can finally exhale. Alisha Yvonne, author of *Loving you is Wrong*, girl, I can not thank you enough. Thanks for stepping in during my moments of writer's block and getting my "creative juices" back to flowing. My literary big sister, The Queen of Hip-Hop Fiction, Nikki Turner, thank you for everything. Our time has come and it won't be long before we "Thelma and Louise" the literary game!

To my friends, thanks for keeping me focused. Hell, if it wasn't for you all, I may not have any interesting stories. I never thought I would be so appreciative of all the drama in my life! Lachele Edmonds A.K.A. Wendy Williams, no matter what anybody says, "You don't have a big mouth!" Melanie Camm, thanks for being my personal aesthetician. Thanks to you the old Noxzema regimen has been replaced with a complex five-step program. Meisha Camm, author of *Hidden Intentions,* you're now part of my literary family too. I knew you could do it. To my really mature, locked down, *"Married with Children* housewife friends, Lakicia Mundle and Toya Smith, what the hell made y'all want to get married? Just joking! Congratulations on the new marriages. Can't wait until my day. You guys are daily motivators. To my big sister at heart, Tracey Davis, stop being so damn evil! To my roommate, Sara Schaible, keep the drinks coming and parties going. I'd much rather party than work out and eat healthy food. Sophronia Plum, you are the true meaning of *A Gangster's Girl, A Hustler's Wife,* and all those things Nikki Turner and I write about. No one knows the game better than you! You are definitely *Married to the Game* and living *The Glamorous Life!* Stephanie Cook, there is no one more real than you. Don't change for nobody! Tiffany Duncan, my little sister at heart, I'm so proud of all your accomplishments. Stay focused; when in doubt, just take a look at my past and determine your future. Rovella Williams, with Versus Entertainment, thanks for all the Atlanta connects. Forget P-Diddy, you hold the keys to the city! To my newest additions, Zariah Smith, Christina Mundle, and Cameron Davis, Nichi loves you all. Thanks to these babies, I don't ever have to have any of my own. Deneen Majors of Major Creations Hair Studio, you still keeping my hair tight. I'm all the way in Atlanta, The Hair Capitol, and I am still faithfully keeping my appointments. Damn! You must really be the bomb! To my coworkers, The Nanston Naughty Girls, you all are hilarious! Thanks to you guys, I love coming to work each day. To Karine, the female Dennis the Menace, keep up the mischief. Tamara, Regulators MC represent! Segeeta, what up, Durdee! Lara, "I'll take Conner for $500, please." Larosa, no wonder you're only at work 2 days a week because you're throwing house parties the other 5 days. Lil Island Girl, see ya at the club. Shenikka, let me hurry up and seal this million-dollar deal so I can let you have ten dollars. Kim, you're the quietest beast I know. Sabrina, chill out! The book is finally here! Lisa thanks for being my guardian angel. Some days I couldn't have made it without you. And last but not least, "Nobody better not say nothing bad about Jeannine or Ms. Crystal!"

To my parents, Angela Mc Zeek and Gary Cobb, thanks for encouraging me when I'm down, listening when I'm whining, hugging me when I'm sad, praising me for my accomplishments and reprimanding me when I'm wrong. And most of all, thanks for being so patient and understanding. Don't worry; I'll repay you all soon enough. And it will be something more precious than anything money can buy. How does a husband to finally take care of me and your first grandbaby sound? Wouldn't it be nice to have me out your hair? Mom, that's probably why yours is gray and Dad, that's probably why you hardly have any!

To my little brother, Vincent McZeek, stay focused, buddy. Your day is coming real soon. Yo big sista got your back.

To the strong men in my life, it is a blessing to have you all. My brother at heart, Donate Davis, can I have some money? Can you get me some clothes? You know no matter how much money I make, I'm always going to ask you those questions, right? They say people change, but you've proven the world wrong. There is no friendship as real as yours. To my biggest male fan, Cee, thanks for all the promo and being my personal Patois editor. Aaron Campbell, A.K.A. Belly of Macten Sound, I love you. It took all I had to steal your heart but I finally got it! There have been times when you looked out for me before you even looked out for yourself. That alone says it all. Your heart is bigger than life. Thank you, thank you, and thanks some more. You'll soon be repaid. To Milton James, Jr, A.K.A. Pumpkin, time heals all wounds. Although it has been quite some time, I would like to say I am sorry. You are the original Vegas and I thank you for all experiences good and bad. God allows us to experience things for a reason and I realize my experiences with you were to prepare me for my blessing as an author. Thank you for everything, and I am sorry for turning my back on you.

Finally, to the haters, liars, backstabbers, non-believers, and just plain old miserable, mean people that are so disappointed with themselves that they try to bring me down, God bless you. Poor babies, you all just need a hug...CLOWNS!

PROLOGUE

Ceazia

"Karma is a muthafucker!" I said aloud as I struggled to pull my Louis Vuitton pilot bag from the trunk of my brand new white 745LI. A year ago, Vegas would have been by my side, pulling the luggage from the trunk as I grabbed the shopping bags from the back seat. Unfortunately, this time I was not returning from a week's trip in Cancun, Mexico. Instead, I was headed to the ghettofab runway of the ho stroll, not to be mistaken with the infamous Church Street in Norfolk. It was another night at the strip club for me. The only purpose my Louis Vuitton luggage served at this point was a dance bag to carry my many multicolored strip-tease uniforms. No more Prada sneakers and Versace sets; it was straight stilettos and dance costumes now. It's a damn shame I had to resort to this shit, but a bitch has got do what it takes to stay on top.

I'd been through every hustler in the Tidewater area of Virginia, and there hadn't been one nigga that could hold shit down like Vegas. I even settled for that nigga, Bear, but he couldn't even do half of what Vegas was doing. And he had the nerve to be talking 'bout love and wifing me up. Spish! Nigga, please! Needless to say, it wasn't long before I had to let him go too.

But as we all know, Miss Ceazia Deveraeux must keep her diva status—by any means. So, if that meant I had to shake a leg or two for a minute to do so, so be it. But remember when I tell you it was only temporary. Like every top-notch chick, I had a plan, and I was already executing. This time, shit was a little more risky, but I loved a challenge. This was the true test. We'd see just how far a bomb-ass chick could get with the power of booty and beauty. Hell, if white girls could do it with athletes, why couldn't a sistah do it with niggas from the streets? So, for all that are interested, take note of what I said once before. Baby, sit back take a shot of Patron and enjoy the ride of C's personal roller-coaster. Ain't nothing changed but the drink and the game, so buckle up, big baby!

CHAPTER 1

WHO SAYS I GOT TO STAY IN YOUR HOUSE?

BJ

Bam!

I slammed the door behind me as I rushed outside. "I hate you!" I screamed upstairs to my aunt, who had custody of me for the past twelve years.

My mother was doing time in the Virginia Women's State Prison for child neglect. One night after a three-day stay at the crackhouse, she came home frustrated and shook my little brother to death. She would often come home fien'in' once her monthly welfare check was gone and there was no more money for drugs. This particular time, Momma was so sick that the constant cry of my 5-month-old brother drove her insane.

I was hiding under the table, which faced the bedroom my brother and I shared. My mother couldn't see me because it was extremely dark in the house. We only had candle lighting because the electric company turned off our services due to non-payment. I remember my mom yelling, "Shut up, boy! Shut up!" as she shook my brother until he was silent. Once he was quiet, she laid him on the mattress we had for a bed in the middle of the floor, and she pulled out a cigarette. I peered at her as she left the room to go lie on the couch. It wasn't until then I felt safe enough to come out. I crawled into the bedroom to lie beside my little brother. I cried silently as I touched his still hand.

"Wake up, little Jay. Wake up," I whispered. But there was no response. I wrapped my arm

4

around his little body and fell asleep.

Beep . . . beeep . . . beeeep!

I woke to see red, orange, and yellow flames all around me. It was amazing that I could still see the fire because the air was filled with thick smoke. I panicked once I realized I couldn't breathe. I didn't know where to find my mom and little brother.

"Mommy . . . Mommy!" I yelled frantically as I felt my way to the back door.

I managed to get outside the house, where I saw all my neighbors standing by, looking at the scene, but my mom and little brother weren't out there. It also seemed that no one knew there were people in the house because they all seemed surprised once I came out. As soon as the firemen pulled up, I begged them to save my brother and mother. Within minutes, they were out. They both lay still as the paramedics tried to resuscitate them. My mom came around shortly after, but my brother's body was covered with a white blanket. That was my signal that he was gone. Everyone figured it was from smoke inhalation, but I knew the truth. To this day, no one knows that my mom really killed little Jay. That will be a secret I'll take to my grave.

The only reason my mom was arrested was for child neglect. The neighbors had reported her to child protective services a number of times, and this time, when she fell asleep with a lit cigarette, was the last straw. It didn't take long for the paramedics to realize she was high. She got a fifteen-year sentence to the Women's State Prison, and that's where she'd been for the past twelve years of my life.

In those years, I'd blossomed from a timid 5-year-old kid to a rebellious teen. The constant bickering between my aunt and me let me know she was just about sick of my mess.

"If you hate it here so bad, then leave!" my aunt yelled after me. I could hear her coming down the stairs as her shouts got louder. "Where you gonna go? Don't nobody else want you," she continued to yell as she opened the screen door.

"I hate it here. I'd rather be dead than live here with you," I shouted back. I knew that answer was only going to lead to one thing, but I was so sick of the foul treatment, I didn't even care.

Smack!

My aunt's huge hand swept across my face. "You better watch your damn mouth, little girl. You gettin' a little too hot for your damn pants."

I jumped up without thinking and smacked her back. In matter of seconds, my aunt's 250-pound frame was all over me. I screamed, hoping my grandmother would come to my rescue.

"Grrraaaaaandmaaaaa! Help! She's trying to kill me."

My grandmother was out the door, pulling my aunt off me in no time. I was big for my size, but my 150-pound frame was nothing compared to the strength of that beast.

"I'm packing my bags!" I shouted as soon as I was free. I ran up the stairs.

I pulled out my Polo backpack and stuffed it with toiletries, underclothes, a pair of Daisy Dukes jean shorts, a white wife-beater, slouch socks, and a fresh pair of white Air Force Ones. I planned to stay at my girl Gina's house. Her mom worked the night shift, 7 P.M. to 7 A.M., at the hospital. We would always have a ball at her house. It was right around 6 o'clock, so I knew her mom would already be out the crib and on her way to work.

"I'm out," I yelled one last time as I ran back down the stairs.

"BJ." I could hear my grandma yelling.

That was the nickname the family had given me. My name is actually Jasmine and everyone called me Jay, but when my brother was born, he was named Javon, and we called him Jay too. So, to distinguish who was who, they began calling us Big Jay and Little Jay. Eventually, Big Jay turned into BJ.

"Yes, Grandma?" I stopped at the back door to hear her out.

"Don't go out there getting in trouble, ya hear?"

"Okay, Grandma. I'll call you." I loved my grandmother and hated for her to worry, but I just had to do me for the time being. I exited the back door and jumped the fence.

A couple of blocks later, I was in the projects. I was cautious as I walked to Gina's place. I was out of my territory, and there were a lot of chicks that didn't like me out there. I dominated the 12th grade with my fully developed body. I kept my weave tight, nails done, and always had the newest sneakers and hottest gear. Needless to say, all the attention was on me, and not too many girls appreciated it when their boyfriends lusted over me.

MARRIED TO THE GAME

I knocked on Gina's front door. I knew she wouldn't be able to hear me because I could hear the music blasting from her bedroom window.

"Yo, Gina!" I called out.

I unsuccessfully attempted to get Gina's attention as I yelled through the open window. So, then I tried the obvious and twisted the doorknob.

"Open says me!" I said out loud.

The door didn't budge. I guess I didn't possess the magic of the many magicians who say those famous words. I headed toward the back door to get the key Gina always left hidden under the mat. As I grabbed the doorknob to insert the key, I noticed the door was open.

Maybe those magic words work after all. I grinned as I slowly entered the house. When walking through the doorway, I noticed the door frame was broken. A huge knot formed in my stomach as I looked around. I wasn't sure if I should run up the stairs or out the door.

"Gina?" I timidly called my best friend's name.

There was no response. My heart began to race as all type of scenarios ran through my mind. I knew I couldn't leave without checking to make sure Gina was okay. In a desperate attempt for protection, I rushed to the kitchen and grabbed a butcher knife.

It's either do or die, I said silently as I crept up the stairs toward Gina's room, praying that she was okay.

When I got to her bedroom, I busted in, ready to stab the first thing moving.

"Aaaahh!" We both screamed at the top of our

lungs.

"Oh my God, Gina. What the hell are you doing?"

Gina jumped up, pulling the covers over her naked body. The smell of sex and weed filled the room. I laughed at her and Duke as they both struggled to get dressed.

Duke had been a friend of ours since elementary school. He'd gotten into a little trouble and was sent off to South Carolina for a few years, but he began doing big things once he returned. Although he was nineteen before he managed to graduate from high school, no one could take away the fact that he made it through.

Duke and Gina always argued and fought with each other during school and even as kids. They had me convinced they hated each other. I had no idea they were actually doing the nasty. Gina was my girl, but since she conveniently kept this juicy detail from me, I attempted to place shame on her with mockery.

"Ah-ha! I blew y'all spot up! I knew something was up with y'all. Ain't no way in hell two people could hate each other as much as or as long as y'all two have," I said as I continued to laugh.

I noticed Gina didn't think it was funny at all.

"Why didn't you knock first? How the fuck you just gonna run up in my shit, BJ?" Gina got on the defensive.

"Actually, I thought something was wrong with your ass since the back door is damn near off the hinges. I was trying to come to your rescue, bitch!" I snapped back then rolled my eyes.

I figured she was embarrassed that her secret was out. I became kind of jealous myself. I had no idea she was having sex.

Duke took his time getting dressed. I noticed him eyeballing my breasts as he massaged his penis. I gave him a seductive grin and returned the favor as I checked out his nice-sized equipment. I'd never noticed just how sexy Duke was until then.

Duke stood a perfect six feet with washboard abs and flawless chocolate skin. His body was decorated with ink, and each tattoo seemed to lie perfectly, complementing his thug sexuality to the tee. Gina quickly interrupted our flirting session.

"Duke, I think you should leave. I'll call you."

Duke agreed without a fight.

"A'ight, momma," he said before kissing her on the cheek and exiting the room. He gave me one last glance and a nod.

I was flattered, so I quickly responded, "Bye, Duke," and grinned.

Now it was time for me to confront Gina. "I always thought we both were virgins, and that when we decided to have sex, we would let each other know. Why didn't you tell me, Gina? And why the hell is the door jacked-up like that?" I asked question after question.

"Why you all up in my grill, BJ? If you must know, Duke broke the door. We had a heated argument earlier in the day and I'd been ignoring his calls, so he decided to come over, but I wouldn't let him in. And you know Duke and his temper. It didn't take but one warning. He told me one time if I didn't open the door, he would kick it in. Although I know his ass is crazy, I didn't think he would actually kick my mom's door in. Well . . . as you can see, he's even crazier than I thought," Gina explained as she shook her head.

I had to shake my head as well. "That boy is a damn fool," I said, although the thought kinda turned me on.

"So, I guess that heated argument quickly turned into make-up sex, huh?" I said sarcastically to force the conversation in the direction I wanted it to go.

Gina obviously answered the simplest question first in hopes I would forget the rest. But oh no! There was no getting out of this one.

Gina looked away as she answered. "I haven't been a virgin for a long time, BJ, but the first time was out of my control. I wish I could tell you more about it, but I can't." I could see Gina wipe the tears from her eyes. I hugged her tightly.

"You can tell me anything, Gina. I won't think any different of you. You're my girl." I tried to reassure her as we talked.

Gina still refused to share. I figured it was either too embarrassing or too hurtful for her to share, so I left the situation alone and allowed her to cry. After minutes of silent tears, Gina finally spoke. "It was Bubba, BJ. It was Bubba." She forced the words out between a huge cry. Bubba was Gina's mother's boyfriend. I couldn't believe what my ears were hearing.

"Bubba? You had sex with Bubba?" I asked.

"Yes. One night he came home drunk after the club. Of course my mom was at work, so I was here alone. He came in my room and started to pull my pajamas off, forcing his hands inside me." Gina stopped in the middle of her statement and began to cry. It was too unbearable to speak about.

"Its okay, Gina. You don't have to say anymore." I hugged her. I could feel her pain. I never experienced being raped, but I'm sure it has to be a painful experience.

"He raped me, BJ. He raped me, and my mother called me a liar when I told her about it. I don't know what hurt more, the rape or my mother's disbelief."

I had no idea Gina had so much pain and hurt inside. There were no words that could heal the pain she felt, so instead of speaking, I just listened and consoled her as she released all the misery she held inside. The room was silent as we sat on her bed. I listened to her constant sniffle as I rubbed her back.

"Its okay, Gina. It's okay," I said softly between rubs. I laid her head on my shoulder and hugged her tight. At that point, I knew not only did I have to do something to get out of my grandmother's home, but I had to get Gina out of her mother's home as well. We were both alone. Although Gina had a mother, she was no longer in her heart. Her mother had deceived her and chose a man over her. And my mother had deceived me in an equal way. It was at that point I made a personal vow. No matter what it took, I would get us both out of this situation. As soon as the opportunity arose, I was jumping aboard, and there was nothing anyone could do to stop me.

CHAPTER 2

I'M A LITTLE SOLDIER IN TRAINING

MARRIED TO THE GAME

Duke

Sex with Gina was always good, but I really wanted to hit BJ. I could tell she wanted me from the way she looked at me. She said she was still a virgin, and I knew her pussy was steaming for some sex. I was just the man to give it to her, too. I wasn't going to rush it, though. I was gonna hit it and I knew it. I was a Jackson man, and we were known for getting any females we wanted. My uncles, Vegas and Snake, ran all the ladies before Vegas was killed. In fact, it was Vegas's womanizing ways that got him murdered. I planned to follow right in my uncles' footsteps, but I'd be much wiser with my shit.

Since moving from South Carolina to Virginia, I'd received constant training from my Uncle Snake about the game, and for the past two years, he'd kept me tight in all the hottest gear and jewelry. Snake had been caught-up in the game for a long time now, and his money was long enough to do things the average nigga would never be able to do. He even bought me a car before I had a driver's license.

Snake liked doing things for me because he always referred to me as his little soldier in training. I knew soon I'd have a piece of the empire and would be doing big things just like him. I began to lay out all my plans. I could see myself with a dope-ass house like Snake's, all the luxury vehicles, and the utmost respect from other ballerz in the game.

One night, I called Snake to see what he was

14

up to, and he told me we needed to go out so we could cover strip club etiquette. I arrived at Snake's house around 10 o'clock, and I was greeted at the door by his girl, Danielle.

Danielle Stevens was this fine-ass, bourgeois chick my uncle met at Hampton University just before he was leaving the campus after serving some boys there. Danielle's mother was a doctor and her father was a lawyer, just like some shit straight off the *Cosby Show*. She was never exposed to the streets before hooking up with my uncle, and that's what she loved about Snake; his spontaneous bad-boy traits. She longed to be "a gangster's girl." Like the other women caught-up in the game with their men, Danielle loved the excitement and all the financial perks that came along with lovin' a gangster.

Danielle was definitely a dime piece. She had a butterscotch complexion, hair down her back, and a small waist with a big ass—just the way I like them.

"What's up, Danielle?" I asked as I admired her phat-ass booty on the way in.

"Hey, Duke. What's going on?" she asked, wondering what the night might bring.

"I don't know, momma. I think we're going to hit the strip joint up tonight."

Danielle's face instantly turned evil as she darted her eyes in Snake's direction. She hated when Snake went to the strip club. All she could think about were the sexual rendezvous he used to have with his stripper ex-girlfriend, Mickie, and her female lover, Sonya, who also enjoyed the erotic lifestyle. The shit my uncles used to do back in the day was wild. No one liked to talk about all that came with their game because it turned into a deadly love triangle, but me, I love it and plan to live it. I stood and watched as Danielle vented.

"Oh, you're going to the strip club tonight, Snake?" Danielle asked him.

"Nah, baby. I don't know why you always let Li'l Soldier get in your head. He knows you hate it when I go there, and that's why he said the shit. Li'l Soldier, stop fucking with my woman's head. You know she ain't cool with hearing about me at no strip club." Snake quickly spit game to Danielle as he took his last pull on the blunt, filled with purple haze.

Spitting game came second nature to my Uncle Snake. It was amazing how easily he could turn things around. Runnin' game was a science, and I had almost mastered it as well as my uncle. I never took notes well in school, but since I had a passion for the game, I made sure not to miss a lesson from Snake. I tried to make Danielle feel like she couldn't take a joke.

"Damn, Danielle, I didn't know you let a young nigga like me get in your head like that. My uncle better watch out," I said with a smirk on my face.

Danielle was not pleased with our taunting. She rolled her eyes and began to clean up the small mess my uncle left behind.

"He thinks I'm fucking stupid. Yeah, keep taking my kindness for weakness. I'm just keeping my composure for the moment as I observe all that's going on around me. But just wait until I catch his ass. Y'all think just because I come from a good background that I won't serve a nigga about playing with me, but try me and you'll find out that shit's going to really hit the fan."

I could hear Danielle mumbling underneath her breath as she cleaned. I walked over and whispered in her ear as my uncle grabbed his keys. "You better watch your mouth, girl," I said in a seductive yet teasing manner.

"We out, baby girl," Snake said as he smacked Danielle's ass then kissed her on the lips.

"Whatever," she responded while rolling her eyes.

She followed Snake to the door. I could see the outline of her thong through her sheer robe as I followed close behind her. Looking at Danielle's ass shake through that robe made my dick hard.

"We out, baby girl," I said, mocking my uncle then smacking her on the ass, causing it to jiggle.

They both laughed, but it wasn't a joke at all. I was planning to fuck that fat ass from the back one day soon. *It may take a while, but I'll get it,* I thought. I winked at her while licking my lips, and grabbed my dick, giving it a gentle massage before closing the door behind me. I was sure then that Danielle knew exactly what was up.

We jumped in Snake's Denali and headed to the strip club. I was a little excited, but I knew I had to play it cool as we pulled up. I followed Snake past security and into the club. That was the first lesson.

I made a mental note: *Get familiar with security. Give them a nice amount of cash to avoid lines and searching.*

Once we were inside, the first stop was the bar, to see who the bartenders were for the night. After determining everything was straight with whoever would be fixing his drinks, he then led me to a spot in the corner near the exit. He beckoned for the waitress and handed her a generous amount of money as he gave orders.

"Courvoisier, and keep 'em coming," he told the skinny, half-dressed woman. Maybe with a few more pounds and an ass, she could have qualified as a stripper versus a waitress.

That was several lessons in one. Snake walked right in without much noise and went over to the bar to make sure he was familiar with the bartenders, just in case someone in the game might be trying to set him up by slipping a mickie in his drinks. Then he headed to a spot near the exit. This was so he could watch everyone who entered and exited the club, without them even noticing him. Also, sitting near an exit made it easy for a quick escape if necessary.

Next mental note: *You must always be aware of your environment so that there aren't any surprises.*

I also liked how Snake paid the bartender and waitress up-front with a generous amount. That kept him from having the hassle of flagging them down and constantly having to place drink orders.

We chilled in the corner for about forty-five minutes. At first that was cool because I was checking out some of the amazing things those chicks could do on that pole, but after a while, the entertainment was no longer holding my attention.

CHUNICHI

Females were coming over left and right asking for a dance, and Snake was turning them down just as fast as they were coming. Now that part of the lesson I didn't grasp at all.

"Unc, why you dissing all the honeys?" I asked.

"A couple of reasons, man. First, some of them are tricks, and we don't do tricks. And second, if you ignore them and act uninterested towards the hot bitches, the challenge is going to make them want you even more. You see, the hot bitches are used to getting any nigga they come at. If you're that one nigga that don't budge, then they're going to want you even more. You feel me, li'l nigga?"

My uncle was so good with game it was ridiculous. Everything he said made perfect sense. I knew to pay close attention when he talked, because I knew everything would prove worthy in days to come.

"I feel you, Unc. I feel ya," I replied.

We continued to chill for another twenty minutes before Snake led me to the velvet room. Shit in there was set-up like a little Egyptian paradise, and the women were beautiful—nothing but top-notch females. These women had perfect tans and flawless bodies. I couldn't find one who didn't have her makeup in check. I could tell they were wearing that expensive shit because they each looked like movie stars. I, for one, was impressed with how much class these ladies carried.

There was one female in particular who kept looking our way. She was the baddest chick in there. She had beautiful caramel skin, a small waist, C-cup breasts and long black hair. Snake noticed me checking her out.

"You like that?" he asked as he waited for a reaction.

I was sure not to seem too pressed. "So far, she's the baddest chick I've seen in here," I carefully responded.

"Each day you show more and more traits like your Uncle Vegas," Snake said as he laughed.

He shook his head as if to say, "It's a pity," then he continued. "She's venomous, man. That's the infamous Ceazia," he said, looking her five-foot-five inch frame up and down.

"Damn, that's her? She doesn't look much like a murderer to me," I said as I watched her move her body like a snake.

Ceazia began to put on a show for me and my uncle as we both plastered our eyes on her. I tried not to show it, but I was about to drool all over myself. This chick had a spell on me that seemed unbreakable. It was tough not letting it show.

I never had a chance to meet Ceazia before, but I'd heard the many tales, and from the looks of things, each story was true. The five years I did in the juvie in South Carolina really had me missing out on a lot. Her panther eyes continued to hypnotize me as she walked over.

"Who's this little one, Snake?" she asked, rubbing her hand across my goatee.

"Nobody you gettin' close to, bitch," Snake snapped at her.

It was never proven that Ceazia was the shooter the day my Uncle Vegas, Mickie, and

Sonya were killed, but Snake was sure she did it.

"Don't be jealous, daddy. You'll always have my attention," she said to Snake as she rubbed his penis. Snake didn't respond. He just looked her coldly in her eyes and knocked her hand away from his manhood.

I couldn't understand how Snake could avoid Ceazia's spellbinding ways. There I sat, wishing she'd touch me again, especially in the crotch area like she'd just touched Snake, but he wasn't fazed by anything Ceazia did or said.

I constantly watched Ceazia throughout the night. The enchantment she had on the men in the club was crazy. I knew she had to be making the most bank in the club. Hell, I was ready to give her all the loot I had in my pockets. I guess it was a good thing my Uncle Snake was there to keep me from making a fool of myself.

I stared intensely. There wasn't a flaw on Ceazia's body. Her skin was perfect, stomach tight, not a stretch mark in sight, and she had perfect white teeth. She was truly a stunner. No wonder my Uncle Vegas was whipped. Pretty soon, I planned to see just how much we really had in common.

CHAPTER 3

FLY ON THE WALL

UNKNOWN MAN

I'd been watching Ceazia's every move as I sat in a dark corner of the strip club where she worked. That bitch had no idea I was even here. She was so busy flirting and spitting game to niggas, she didn't even notice me nearly breathing down her fucking neck. All Ceazia saw was dollar signs. Unless you were frosted from ear to belly button, that's earring to chain, and had on an outfit totaling at least $500, a nigga could forget it. I'd told her time and time again, she needed to stay on point. But ever since she got away with Vegas' shooting, she felt like she was on top of the damn world, and could let her guard down at any time. And these cats constantly blowing her head up didn't make shit no betta. This chick truly carried it like she was the Diamond Princess. But like I always told her, once in the game, you're married to the game. At any time, a nigga could be breathing down her neck, ready for revenge, ready to snatch her off that throne.

I continued to watch as she flirted with Snake, and even his li'l nigga, Duke. The effect she had on niggas was stupid! Although I hadn't seen her or even spoken to her in over a month, she was still as fine as the first day I met her. That girl meant the world to me. I would give her my last chicken wing, my last dollar, and even my last breath if I had to, just to please her, but the bitch was just never happy. I would give that bitch my all. It was so many times I fell short on a nigga's money because of her. I even had to buck on niggas and rob a couple of niggas down South just to get back on. Hell, that damn 745 she was driving was bought with a nigga's money I bucked on. And even with all of that, she still wasn't happy. All she kept hollering 'bout was that nigga, Vegas. That man was dead and I still had to compete. But I refused to give up. If I couldn't have her, no one would.

Although Ceazia possessed the most deadly seductive ways that could exist in a woman, I still loved her and yearned for her presence. She could have the most cautious nigga slippin' at any time. It seemed like now she was working on that nigga, Snake. Unfortunately, he looked weak, and seemed to be following real close behind the steps of his late brother. Even though he knew C was guilty of shooting Vegas, and he had all sorts of hatred towards her for it, she still had him weak. I could tell by the look in his eyes. Hell, she even had li'l Duke mesmerized.

Duke was a young buck, so he was easily persuaded, but I thought Snake could stand his ground. I knew C, and if Snake didn't tighten up, he would be her next target. And trust me, that bitch had good aim. She didn't miss a target.

I could only sit back and shake my head as if to say, "It's a pity," as I watch Ceazia get in Snake's brain and send him and his li'l man out the club's door confused.

CHAPTER 4

A SOLDIER'S STRUGGLE

SNAKE

That bitch, Ceazia, had me tripping. Every time I saw her, she came on to me like shit was supposed to be all good. I had every reason in the world to hate her ass, and she knew it. I didn't know why she insisted on trying to play me like a sucker, but in a bit, I'd be the one having the last laugh. In the meantime, I'd just keep running game to her like everything was all good.

Not only did Ceazia murder my brother, but she also murdered my girlfriend, Mickie. That was two too many deaths among people whom I loved, who had to die at the hands of one vicious woman. That bitch was lucky she was still alive. The only reason she was still walking was because there was a lot of evidence pointing in other directions. But personally, I didn't give a fuck. I thought the bitch did it, and as soon as I got it confirmed, she was dead. On that, I put everything I love, from money to hoes to my little soldier, Duke.

"What's on your mind, Snake?" Duke said, noticing that I was deep in thought.

"Nothing, li'l man. Just thinking. Sometimes shit be that way."

"She got you fucked up, huh, Unc? I can see it in your eyes when you look at her."

I began to feel like I taught this nigga a little too well. He started looking closely at my facial expression and could figure out my thoughts. But only a little soldier could do that because he was a reflection of me, and of course, of my late brother Vegas. I messed with his mind a bit.

"What? You think you so good at reading niggas that you can read me too?" I questioned him to shake him up a little.

"Nah, man. That's just how she got me feeling. I mean, I loved Uncle Vegas to death and I want to be just like him, but at the same time, I'm feeling her, and she's the bitch that took him away. It's a struggle, Unc, and I'm fucked up."

I knew exactly how my li'l soldier felt, because it was a struggle I knew all too well. We rode home in silence, both of us deep in thought.

It was three in the morning and Danielle was still up when I arrived home. I knew an argument was in store. Lately, she was acting insecure, and it led to constant fighting. I hollered at Duke before he left and took that dreaded walk into the crib. Danielle's face was frowned up as soon as I opened the door. I tried to lighten things up a little because I would much rather fuck than fight.

"Hey, baby. What you still doing up? I expected my woman to be lying in bed, waiting on me once I got home," I stated.

She exploded as soon as I opened my mouth. "What the fuck you think I'm doing up? It's three in the damn morning, and my man is just now getting home! Don't ask me no damn questions. You're the one who got some answering to do. And don't try that sweet-talking shit with me, Snake. If you really wanted me in bed waiting, you woulda brought your ass home before three in the morning!"

Danielle continued screaming as she turned the TV and lights off then headed up the stairs

27

toward the bedroom. That was exactly where I wanted her—in the bed. I figured I'd let her vent a while, then give her the dick. I followed her up the stairs with a fake plea.

"Come on, baby girl. You know I have to take care of business. How else will you be able to prance around in your Chanel slippers and lingerie? Don't I always come through for you? Baby girl, I try to keep things on the level so you don't have to want for shit. Why can't you understand that all of a sudden?"

I always used the game as an excuse for being out late, even though niggas knew I didn't do business after ten at night. It didn't look like she was buying it this time, though. Danielle continued fussing, not letting up one bit.

"Why the fuck was your phone off? I paged you five times. You're so fucking inconsiderate when you don't answer my calls. You never know what's wrong, or even if I have something urgent to tell you. If I ever ignored you or turned my phone off, you'd be ready to beat my ass. And you know what—that's what I should do to you right now. There's no way in hell you couldn't have known I tried to reach you. I even hit you up with a two-way message . . . blah . . . blah . . . blah . . . blah . . ."

After about one minute of continuous yelling, I tuned Danielle out completely. I realized I may not be getting any ass after all, so I had to resort to plan B. I told her I was headed to take a cold shower then began to get undressed. I noticed Danielle's eyes watching my every move. She continued to complain, but her tone lowered with every stitch of clothing I let fall to my feet. Working out daily to keep my body tight paid off during times like this between me and Danielle. I knew she'd begin to think twice after taking a look at my rock-hard abs, but this wasn't the only part of me that bared stiffness. Danielle's eyes traveled just a short way south of my waistline and focused intently on the piece of me she could appreciate the most.

Once all of my clothes were off, I began stretching as if I were tired. I used this opportunity to flex my muscles as Danielle looked on. By then her tone had completely softened, and I had her just where I wanted. The table had taken a sudden turn, and the ball was now in my court. I gave her a humble look and shook my head. Then I spoke to her softly.

"You win, baby. You win. I don't want to argue," I said, walking over to put my arms around her waist.

I kissed Danielle gently on her neck. I knew her pussy would be throbbing in a matter of seconds, because such teasing always worked after a fight between Danielle and me. I continued to the bathroom, intentionally leaving the door open for a small tease. I turned off the vanity lights over the mirror, leaving only the dimmed lights over the shower. The setting couldn't have been more perfect for an erotic mood.

I jumped in the shower, opting for steaming hot water over cold, since I was now on top and things were pointing towards sex again. I took my time standing under the massaging shower head. Stress slowly left my body with each drop of water that hit my back and shoulders. I soon noticed a shadow against the shower door. I could see that it was the silhouette of Danielle's perfect body.

Danielle opened the shower door and began to kiss me passionately. I reached to lift her into the shower without ever losing the lock between our lips. Water ran down our faces as we kissed. The water soaked Danielle, causing her sheer robe to cling to her wet body. The scene of her soaking wet hair, clothes, and body turned me on. She was so sexy standing before me submissively.

I quickly disrobed her and lifted her 125-pound frame against the shower wall, fondling her pussy with my fingers. The wetter she became, the harder my dick became, so without hesitation, I inserted my penis into her slippery vagina. She moaned with pleasure while scratching my back. I gently sucked her neck with each stroke coming closer to ejaculation.

"Aaaahh!" We both yelled as we came together.

That was all I needed, and it was time for bed. We climbed into bed together, and I watched ESPN as I pulled on my last few puffs of a blunt. I was trying to quit smoking, but I had to at least start my day off and end it with a smoke, if nothing else.

Just as I was getting relaxed and Danielle was off to sleep, she was awakened when my phone began to ring.

"Who the fuck is that calling you this late, Snake? I know you ain't got no hoes calling you at this time of morning, while you're laying up next to me!" Danielle yelled.

The caller had awakened the dragon. The yelling was like her spitting fire at my ass. I reached over to the nightstand and pressed end without even looking at the caller ID, and sent the caller to voicemail. I looked over at Danielle, and she looked as if she was ready to tag me, but she soon rolled her eyes and lay back down. Ten minutes later, she was awakened by the song "PIMP" by 50 Cent.

"Damn, it's a message on my sidekick. Who the hell is tripping this late?" I whispered to myself.

I knew it couldn't be an emergency because whoever it was would have called my crib. I flipped open the phone to check the email. It read: COME SEX ME. It was signed SWEET SIXTY-NINE. Whoever this was, they were truly tripping. I turned the phone off and lay back down. I looked to see what Danielle was doing, and she was staring me in my face as soon as my head hit the pillow.

"What, Danielle? What?" I asked. She was really starting to piss me the fuck off.

"What you mean 'what?' Who the hell was that? And be sure to answer carefully, Snake, because you know I ain't no fool."

I really didn't feel like arguing. I stared Danielle in the eyes with a "c'mon now" look, which bought me some time to think, and then I lied.

"It's my li'l soldier, Duke. He just got some ass. You know how he does when he hit," I said convincingly.

Vegas and I had a tradition. Each time one of us would get some ass that we'd been working at

31

for a while, we would hit each other on the text message and type in GOT 'EM as a signal that we finally got the panties. When Duke began his soldier training, this is something I passed down to him as well.

At first, Danielle's face seemed as if she didn't want to accept that excuse, but she finally threw her hands up in the air and went back to sleep.

The next morning, I went out on the balcony to have my morning smoke and chill before starting my day. The breeze from the river was cool. I decided to check my voicemail to see if the strange caller from last night left a message. I had one message, and it was the sound of a female masturbating. I must say it sounded good too. In fact, it sounded so good it made my dick rise. I had no idea who the woman could be, but if she looked as good as she sounded, she wouldn't have to worry about sending e-mails or leaving voice messages anymore.

As I listened to the message, I began to feel as though someone was standing over me. I turned around and Danielle was standing at the sliding door, looking through the curtains at me. She was really starting to scare me. The look in her eyes was like a fatal attraction. I figured I better chill out because I wasn't trying to end up like my brother, Vegas.

CHAPTER 5

HOT SEX ON A PLATTER

MARRIED TO THE GAME

GINA

BJ had been my girl since pampers, but I just couldn't tell her when I lost my virginity. I was glad I finally had the chance to talk to her about it, though. However, I didn't really tell her everything. It was tough talking about the day I lost my virginity, so I kept things brief.

Ever since I began having sex two years before, at age sweet sixteen, I'd had an urge to sex all men—big, small, short and tall. I never had sex with guys in my school or my neighborhood, though. That's how I'd been able to keep my promiscuous ways a secret for so long. Besides, guys didn't talk as much as girls, so as long as those boys didn't know each other, my fast ways stayed hidden.

Despite the fact that I took all the necessary precautions, I still wasn't able to keep anything from Duke. He was like a bloodhound when it came to sniffing out females that were giving it up. When Duke and I finally got together, I was like a bitch in heat. I loved every minute of him sexing me.

BJ was around a lot since she got into it with her aunt. As a result, Duke and I couldn't have sex that often. She was seriously throwing salt in my game. So, my sex drive was now in fifth gear, and I needed some bad. Fortunately, BJ's fine-ass cousin Ray-Ray had been around just as much as her, and I began to feel him a whole lot. There was no resisting this six-foot tall black stallion. He had tiger eyes that hypnotized at first glance, and muscles that bulged as thick as the knots of money in his pockets.

We were all chilling, smoking, and watching movies when Ray-Ray started to make his move.

"Damn, girl!" he yelled as I bent my 24-inch waistline over and mooned him, showing my soft golden ass as I changed the DVD.

I knew the sight of my tender,18-year-old ass hanging out would get his attention, if nothing else did. I pretended as if I didn't know what his sudden outburst was about.

"Damn, girl, what?" I asked, trying to be nonchalant.

It was hard to keep from laughing with BJ on the couch, constantly snickering. BJ was my girl, and she'd seen me in action before, so she knew exactly what I was up to.

"You know what the hell I'm talking 'bout. You keep putting that shit in my face, and I'm gon' do something to yo' ass," Ray-Ray threatened.

That's exactly what I wanted to hear. Now it was time to call his bluff. I pulled my terrycloth shorts up in my ass to resemble a thong, and started to sway back and forth in his face. He stood up and grabbed me by my butt cheeks, pulling me close to his body. Then he whispered in my ear.

"I'm man enough to see what you tryna do, girl. Let's go upstairs."

I looked back at BJ for approval. She shrugged then smiled, so I knew it was cool. I looked at Ray-Ray with a huge grin.

"Let's go," I said, grabbing him by his hand and

leading him up the stairs.

When we entered the room, he immediately threw me on the bed. He was much rougher than Duke, but I didn't mind. I knew this was going to be excitingly different, so I pulled off my shorts without hesitation.

Our forceful foreplay was interrupted by a knock at the front door. I looked out the window and saw Duke. I tried to ignore the knock, praying that he would assume I wasn't home and go away.

Duke began to bang more forcefully. Again I tried to ignore it. I grabbed Ray-Ray by the neck and began to kiss him passionately. I wanted him, and by all means I was going to have sex with him. Eventually, there was no more sound at the door. I was relieved that Duke had left. I turned the stereo on and watched Ray-Ray as he got undressed. His body was nice, his skin was smooth like silk, and his six-pack was very defined. His body was just as perfect as Duke's. I figured if the sex was as good, I may have two dicks to screw instead of one.

"Ray-Ray . . . Ray-Ray!" I couldn't help screaming his name as he sexed me.

He was right about doing something to me. He didn't make love to me, he fucked me, and I loved it. My hormones were raging, and Ray-Ray's dick was right on time.

After sex, we smoked a blunt to bring down the adrenaline rush. Soon after smoking, Ray-Ray fell asleep. I went downstairs to check on BJ. She was asleep on the couch in the same place I left her.

"BJ." I shook her shoulder.

She opened her eyes slowly.

"What's up, girl?"

"Did you answer the door when Duke came over?" I asked her, so I could get my lie together.

"Yeah, I did. I told him you were sleeping, though." That was a perfect answer. That was a lie that needed no elaboration.

"Okay, that's cool. I'm going to call him now while Ray-Ray is sleeping."

"Damn, girl, you put him to sleep?" BJ looked excited at the thought.

I knew she was itching for the day that she could be in my shoes. Happy about the envy, I decided to rub her nose in my experience a little.

"Yeah, girl. The dick was real good, too. You mean to tell me you couldn't hear us up there? I put it on his ass, and he stuck it to me too. He really knows how to work it. You'll experience it all in due time, though."

BJ gave me an unusual smirk at that statement. "I'm almost sure I will," she responded sarcastically.

I guess I began to really get under her skin, so I decided to lay off the sex talk for a while. I only wanted to keep her envious enough to wonder about a sex life before she actually started to indulge.

There was another knock at the door as I headed upstairs.

"BJ, can you get that?" I yelled from the top of the stairs.

BJ opened the door. I could see her conversing with someone. She leaned back and said, "It's Duke. He won't leave. He says he knows you're here. He heard you yelling for me to get the door."

"Damn. Ray-Ray is upstairs. What am I going to do?" I said softly as I came down the stairs toward the door. At first I thought to go and wake Ray-Ray before letting Duke in, but BJ opened the door sooner than I was ready.

Duke's face was balled up as he walked toward me. He grabbed my arm firmly as he let me know how upset he was at me.

"What the fuck is up with you? What type of games you playing, Gina?"

I couldn't think of a lie fast enough, so I just remained silent. BJ stepped in to rescue me.

"Chill out, Duke. You that damn pussy-whipped that you gotta act all crazy and shit?" She pulled his ego card and it worked.

He let my arm go with a quickness. Niggas don't like when women test their manhood.

"You must be sick in your head, female. I don't get whipped. It's just the principle. I don't like to be disrespected."

BJ gave Duke that same unusual, mischievous smirk she'd given me earlier and stated, "Don't speak too soon. You haven't had *all* pussy, so you don't know if you could be whipped or not."

Once again, Duke eyeballed BJ's voluptuous body and grabbed his dick, giving it a small massage. The other day when he did that, I thought maybe I was hallucinating, but this time I was sure I was not.

"What the fuck are you doing, Duke? Why you rubbing your dick and shit?" I called him out.

"Come on, Gina, don't trip. You know I always

do that shit," he answered without emotion.

Just then, Ray-Ray came walking down the stairs.

"What up, fam," he said as he dapped Duke up.

I was in a real fucked up predicament. Ray-Ray hugged me.

"A'ight, Gina," he said then walked over to BJ and hugged her.

"A'ight, li'l cuz."

I was afraid to even look at Duke. I had no explanation. I didn't answer the door when he came over, and then a nigga comes out my room.

"You fucking that nigga, too?" he asked, laughing. "I guess word on the streets is true. You give that ass up quicker than a broke fiend trying to get a fix," Duke stated as he headed for the door.

I grabbed him, trying my best to explain. He wasn't trying to hear anything I had to say, though.

"It's all good, shortie. There's no hard feelings. I'll be over some other time to hit that ass." He smacked my butt before pulling out his cell and making a call.

"Yo, Veronica. I'm on my way," I could hear him saying as he walked away.

CHAPTER 6

SLEEPING WITH THE ENEMY

CEAZIA

Each night when I came home there were so many things that reminded me of Vegas. I should have sold the house just like I sold his car, clothes, and jewelry after his death, but I just couldn't give it up. I worked too hard and went through too much for that house to just let it go. I held Vegas down during his jail sentence, I did time for a crime I didn't even commit, and was harassed by his mistress while doing it. Hell, I deserved everything I had—and Vegas, Mickie, and Sonya deserved what they got too. Anyone else in my shoes would have done the same thing.

Imagine coming home after serving five hard months in jail for a crime you didn't commit and finding *your* man, in *your* house, in *your* Jacuzzi, having a threesome with one of *your* best friends and her lover. That was definitely a death sentence. I had to do it. Luckily, I moved slowly and carefully, and that's why I was on the streets now.

Although I didn't regret a thing I'd done, I must admit things hadn't been the same without Vegas. But I'd learned to cope with it. Every night I was at the strip club just to hold shit down. That little bit of money wasn't worth the aggravation. I'd done all I could to get back on top, but it just wasn't happening. I was fucking with this nigga from up top, another from the dirty south, and even that nigga, Bear, that Vegas used to cop his raw from; and all these niggas together, combined with me stripping, still couldn't compare to how Vegas was putting out. It seemed like I was going to have to go for what I knew, and keep it in the family. I'd checked out how that bitch, Danielle, was living, and it seemed like it was pretty well. So, if Snake could do for her, I knew he could do even more for a bitch like me.

As much as I hated to do it, Snake was about to be the next nigga to catch my heart. Hey, desperate times called for desperate measures. I made it my personal goal to get Vegas's brother, Snake. I had been reeling him in slowly. I could tell by the look in his eyes that he wanted me too. It took all he had to fight the attraction. I'd ended each night with a voice message on his phone or a text on his Sidekick. Tonight, I would leave another text.

I walked over the computer to check my e-mail before sending Snake a message. To my surprise, there was a return message from him. It read: STOP PLAYING THE GAMES. MAKE YOURSELF KNOWN. THAT MASTURBATION SOUNDS GOOD, BUT I THINK YOU COULD USE MY HELP.

That was perfect. At least I had him involved in the game. He was curious to find out who I was. I replied: THE GAME IS OVER. MEET ME AT YOUR REGULAR STRIP SPOT ON THURSDAY AT YOUR REGULAR TIME. I'LL HIT YOU UP WHEN I'M READY.

I was sure my plan was going to work. All I needed was one night with him, and he would be trapped. The power of the pussy is phenomenal.

Thursday came in no time. I headed to the club

in a hurry. I wanted to be sure I beat Snake there. I purchased new costumes, got a beautiful golden tan, got my hair, nails, and eyebrows done and put on my MAC makeup to perfection. I must say I was gorgeous. I didn't give any dances the entire night. I wanted to be fresh for Snake. I had a new routine choreographed especially for him.

Around midnight, he walked in the velvet room. He took his usual seat. That was my cue. I signaled the DJ to play R Kelly's "Snake." That was the perfect song considering my target. I slithered all over the stage, up and down the pole, with my eyes fixed on Snake the entire time. He didn't take his eyes off me either. He licked his lips while staring at me seductively. Just the look on his face was making my juices flow.

After the song ended, I went to the dressing room to freshen up and change costumes. Snake was still sitting in the same spot when I returned. I walked up to him, straddled his lap, and whispered in his ear. "This one is on the house."

Then I gave him the lap dance of his life. I started with a slow wind on his lap. I ran my fingers through his hair as I moved my vagina in a circular motion on his penis. I loved men with hair. Luckily, Snake had his hair out instead of his usual cornrows. I did every position imaginable for a lap dance. I didn't stop until I felt his manhood grow. Once I felt the magic stick, I knew I had him exactly where I wanted him. I ended the dance, kissed him on the cheek, and returned to the dressing room.

"Mission accomplished," I said as I flopped on

the couch to catch my breath.

I took a shower and put on my regular clothes, then headed out of the club. I went to my car and called Snake's phone.

"Yo," he answered.

"Meet me outside. Just go to your truck," I instructed before hanging up.

I was sure by this time Snake knew I was his secret admirer. I listened to the radio as I waited. Five minutes passed and he still wasn't out. I looked toward his truck to be sure he wasn't already in there waiting. I noticed a strange person dressed in black looking through his truck. I wasn't sure if it was a detective or someone plotting to rob him, but I wasn't getting involved. I leaned back in my seat so that I would not be labeled as a witness. A few moments later, I heard Snake talking to one of the bouncers as he headed to his truck. Once he got in, I walked over. He looked at me and hesitantly unlocked the door.

"So, you're Sexy Sixty-nine?" he asked as I climbed in the truck.

"Yep. You disappointed?" I said sarcastically.

"Do I look disappointed?" he answered with a question.

Honestly, I could not read him at all. I wasn't sure what he was thinking.

"Guess not."

"Good. So, where we headed?" Snake put the truck in reverse.

I wanted to go back to my place, but I was afraid it may be too much for Snake to handle. I totally remodeled the bedroom, so it didn't even resemble the old one. The crime scene was too much for me to handle as well. The old bedroom was a constant reminder of the murders. I decided to take my chances with the house.

"You can go to my crib," I said cautiously.

He looked uncertain, but agreed. A few minutes later we were at my house. I punched in the code and we entered the gate. I jumped out of the truck and headed to the door. When I unlocked it, I noticed Snake still sitting in the truck.

"Come on in," I yelled.

He just sat there, shaking his head.

"I can't do it, ma," he responded.

I guess my house wasn't the best choice after all. But I wasn't giving up. I didn't live far from the beach, and there were plenty of hotel options on the oceanfront. I headed back to the truck.

"It's cool. I understand. Let's get a room at the beach."

We pulled out of the gate and headed back out. That was close. I thought that may have ruined the night, so I had to get back to horny. I began to rub his inner thigh, working my way toward his penis. He still seemed to be distracted and unmoved. I was sure Vegas was on his mind, and if I didn't think fast, the night would come to an abrupt end. I had no choice. I had to suck his dick.

I popped in a cough drop and unzipped his pants. I gently pulled out his penis and massaged it with my tongue, making sure I got it nice and moist. I didn't want to take the chance of starting a fire, jerking a dry dick. Giving head wasn't my specialty, but I could get the job done. My goal was not to make him cum, but to get him back in the mood.

Snake moaned with pleasure as he rubbed his hand through my hair. Eventually, my rhythm was guided by the pressure of his hand forcing my head up and down.

It didn't take long for us to arrive at the hotel. I was relieved when we arrived because my jaws were getting rather tired. We stopped at the front desk, and minutes later we had a room. We quickly headed to our suite. The entire way, Snake's phone and Sidekick were constantly going off. Each time he would press end, sending the caller to voicemail. That was the best option Nextel could have ever come up with.

I was eager to get a taste of that loving Mickie had often bragged about. I hurried to get the mood right. I turned on the radio, turned off the lights and cracked the balcony door so we could hear the waves crashing against the shore. The room came with chilled champagne, so I popped open the bottle and poured us both a glass. Drunken sex was always the best sex, so a little alcohol wouldn't hurt. After we finished the last glass of champagne, Snake pulled out a blunt.

"I have to hit this before I do anything. It takes the drunken edge off. You wanna hit?" he offered.

"Hell nah!" I instantly refused.

Drugs were no longer part of my diet. A couple of years ago I would have had my own personal stash, but not any more. I'd seen the effects of drugs; they cost Vegas his life. I took my last smoke that day, and I've been drug free ever since.

CHUNICHI

As soon as Snake finished smoking he began to undress. I started to unbutton my shirt and he grabbed my arms and pinned them to the bed. He got on top of me and began to suck and bite my neck. He snatched my shirt open, popping the buttons off.

"You want this dick?" he asked.

"Yes, give it to me," I begged.

He continued to pull my clothes off, tearing my panties and bra. Then he stopped moving completely.

"You don't want it," he said.

I figured he wanted me beg, so I played along.

"Please give it to me, Snake. Fuck this pussy."

That must have given him the drive he needed because he lifted me off the bed, rolled on his back, and straddled me across his lap.

"Well, show me then," he said as he sat me on his big black handle, which resembled a king-sized Snickers.

Boy, did he and Vegas have a lot in common. We had sex in every position one could think of. By the time we finished, my body was sore and bruised. The sex we had was nothing like the passionate lovemaking experiences Mickie would speak about. Our sex was quite opposite. It was rough, hard, and sweaty. Snake didn't caress me, kiss me, or take it slow. In fact, there were times when he would choke me, pull my hair, and even smack me.

I asked him about the difference as I lay on the bed, still naked. "Wow! That was a different performance from the stories I've been told."

He looked at me blankly as he got dressed.

"Oh, well. New bitch, new tricks, I guess." He continued to get dressed without even looking at me. He pulled out his Sidekick and began to type. I looked over his shoulders and read: GOT 'EM—OR RATHER SHE GOT ME.

The message was simple. I wasn't sure of the meaning, but I didn't bother to inquire.

"I got to run. How much is a cab going to cost you to get back to the club?" he asked as he laced his brand new wheat-colored Tims.

I couldn't believe this nigga had the audacity to even think I was getting my sexy ass in a cab. I thought maybe I'd misunderstood him, so I asked for clarification.

"Excuse me? Did you ask about a cab?"

"Yeah. How much you need? I don't have time to take you back to the club. I gotta run."

I laughed to keep from snapping off on him. "Honey, I don't do cabs."

"Okay, I'll have my li'l soldier come scoop you," he said as he opened his cell phone.

"Duke, I need you to come to my spot at the oceanfront, room one-twelve, and pick up this chick for me. She'll be going back to the strip joint . . . One."

He closed the phone and headed for the door.

"Can I pencil you in for next week? Same time, same place?" I asked.

"Yeah, hit me up," he said as he closed the door behind him.

I jumped in the shower to clean myself up. As I dried off, I examined myself in the mirror. Snake had been really rough during sex. I had a bruise on my hip, neck and butt cheeks.

I heard a bang on the door. I answered in my towel to entice Snake's li'l soldier a little.

"Hi, Little Soldier," I said as I admired his jewelry.

He wore a rose-gold soldier charm flooded with diamonds. He reminded me so much of Vegas it was ridiculous.

"Little?" he said as he looked at me seductively.

"I'm sorry. Did I offend you?" I asked as I propped my leg on the bed beside him and began to lotion it.

"Do I look like a little boy to you? Tell me one thing on me that reminds you of a little boy."

I looked at him and examined every part of his body. He was about 5 feet 11 inches, so he didn't have the height of a little boy. He didn't have a little boy cut, so that was out. His clothes were the shit, and his jewelry definitely wasn't little boy-like. There was nothing I could readily say, so I took a shot at his manhood.

"Well, from what I can see, there is nothing little boy about you. But there is a lot that I can't see," I said as I looked toward his penis.

"Well, we can solve that now," Duke said as he stood up.

I was interested to see what he was packing, so I didn't stop him. In fact, I encouraged him.

"If it's pleasing, I'll drop my towel and show you what a big girl looks like."

Without hesitation, Duke unzipped his pants, pulled down his boxers and pulled out his penis. I had lost the bet. His johnson was the size of a full-grown man, and it wasn't even hard yet. He knew I was pleased.

"Drop the towel," he demanded as he tugged on the fold just above my breast.

I smiled, un-tucked the towel, and let it drop to the floor.

"Damn, girl," he said as he licked his lips and massaged his penis. I watched it grow with every stroke. I knew I had to end the session before something terrible happened.

"Okay, Little Soldier, you win. Get dressed. I got business to take care of. I'm in a hurry," I said as I threw my clothes on and headed to the door.

He followed behind me, disappointed that I left him hanging—literally.

CHAPTER 7

STILL TAILING THEM

UNKNOWN MAN

"Got 'em!" I said to myself as I watched Snake leave his favorite spot on the oceanfront: the Crown Grand Suites.

I knew it wouldn't be long before he gave in. Although a nigga tried to prepare for the worse, shit still hit hard. The thought of him fucking C has fucked my head up! I had a mind to do some real grimy shit and show them a part of me neither one of them would like to see. My wicked thoughts were distracted as Ceazia came into view.

I watched Ceazia from the crack of her hotel room curtain. Her naked body was still perfect as she walked in the bathroom for a shower. Just the sight of her sexy frame took me back to the many nights we spent in five-star hotels. Our last trip was to Las Vegas, when I watched as she strutted across the hotel floor, modeling her brand new La Perla lingerie. She was like a kid on Christmas that day. We'd hit every designer store Las Vegas had to offer.

Fifteen minutes later, my daydream was over and I focused my attention back on Ceazia's hotel room. She was rushing out of the bathroom draped only in a towel as she headed toward the door. I wondered who could be there as I waited for her to walk back in view.

"Duke? What the hell is he doing there?" I said aloud.

Through the curtain I could see C's freak ass throwing Duke the seduction game. I watched as she teased and taunted him. I could only wonder how long Duke would play along before making a move. Quicker than I'd expected, Duke responded to Ceazia's little game. I couldn't believe my eyes as Duke pulled down his pants and in a single motion, pulled his dick out.

What the fuck! I know she's changed and is playing the survival game, but I never thought this bitch would go this far. She fucking li'l boys and shit now?

My stomach turned as I imagined the unthinkable, Ceazia and Duke fucking. There was no way I could let that shit go down. I jumped out of the car with gun in hand and headed toward the hotel room. I released the safety and cocked the gun back as I positioned myself close to the window for a better aim.

This is it! I thought as I took one final glance into the window. I continued to watch as Duke pulled off Ceazia's towel. I couldn't bear to watch this shit any longer. Sweat began to bead up on my forehead and the pace of my breathing sped up. I swallowed then exhaled as I prepared to put this shit to an end. With gun in hand and fire in my eyes, I looked back at the room one last time before pulling the trigger.

"Whew! That's what's up!" I said to myself as Duke and C exited the hotel room.

I smiled, relieved that they didn't engage in sex. I'd hate to have to knock that li'l nigga off. Although nothing happened this time, I knew it was not over. Knowing my li'l man, fucking C was a personal goal of his, and he wasn't going to stop there. He may not have gotten her this time, but I was sure he was making her an objective. I just hoped C didn't do anything to cause harm to herself or anyone else sooner than expected.

Once I saw Duke and Ceazia pull off, I returned to my car, turned up Jay Z's "99 Problems," and drove off, content.

CHAPTER 8

BEAUTY SHOP GOSSIP

DANIELLE

It was another damn morning that Snake didn't bring his ass home. Once again, his excuse was "I had to do an all-nighter." Today, I wasn't even worried about it. I was doing for Danielle. I had a full day of beautifying. To start the day off, I was going to get my hair done. Normally, I would do my own hair, but I'd been hearing a lot about this young lady in Norfolk by the name of DeeDee. I heard she did all the hottest styles from cornrows to colors to cuts. She did big heads, bald heads, knotty heads, chicken heads—it didn't matter; DeeDee's touch was like magic. Everyone came out of her shop with a nice 'do.

I pulled up to Creative Styles located in the heart of Park Place at 9 A.M. sharp. I circled the block twice to be sure I got a parking spot as close to the shop as possible. I needed to be able to look out the window periodically to keep a constant check on my car. After parking, I grabbed my purse tightly, and pressed the lock button on my keychain and repeated to assure a definite lock. Then I quickly maneuvered my way through begging bums, playing kids, and dangerous drug dealers to get to the doors of the shop.

"Hello, I have a nine o'clock appointment with DeeDee," I told the receptionist as I walked in.

Although the location and outer appearance of the shop was terrible, I was relieved to see the inside was really nice. I must say I was impressed. I took a seat closet to the window and took turns watching television and my car, until it was my turn. I wasn't there ten full minutes before Snake started calling my phone. I sent him directly to voicemail. I had no words for his ass. I had no plans on speaking to him the entire day.

Maybe he'll spend more time at home if I give him a taste of his own medicine, I thought as I constantly pressed the end button on my Baby Phat Nextel phone.

As I waited, I listened to all the different stories the young ladies told. The stylist assistant was a slim girl with huge breasts. She was quite comical as she commented on every statement the young ladies would make. Every so often she would stop in the middle of her conversation, yell out numbers to everyone sitting in the waiting area, and direct them to their proper location by addressing them by their number.

"Girl in the white, you're number one. Beside her—two. Down the row—three, four, five, and six. Now, who all need relaxers . . . color . . . cuts? Okay, number one, sit in my chair and let me base you. Two—to the bowl. Three—be on standby," she yelled then returned to her previous conversation.

By the looks of things, she was running this shop like an assembly line. One slip-up and you were off the line. In the short time I was there, the assistant had already skipped over two clients. One was out taking a smoke break when her number was called, and the other was eating. The shop was packed, and I certainly didn't plan on spending my entire day there. So to prevent that, I turned my attention away from the TV and toward the stylist stations.

I listened alertly as the women talked about different men, baby momma drama, and other types of gossip. I was sure Snake's name would come up, since this area was his stomping ground. Five minutes didn't even pass before I heard it.

"What you getting today?" DeeDee asked the poorly dressed woman that her assistant referred to as number one.

"The works, gurl. Perm, trim, and sew-in," she responded with her ghetto accent.

"Umph. You must have hit the jackpot last night," DeeDee suggested.

"Or turned some tricks," her assistant added underneath her breath.

"No, I did not. My money-maka came in da club last night and broke me off or whateva," the hoochie bragged.

"And what stunts did you have to pull this time—Moet bottle up ya ass?" another one of the girls asked.

"Nah, gurl. I got me a new nigga this week. I told y'all I been plotting, but y'all won't trying to hear a bitch."

Then that's when I heard the ultimate.

"I got dat nigga Snake on my team!" the bitch bragged while rolling her giraffe neck.

"Snake be breaking you off like that?" DeeDee asked in disbelief.

The entire shop was in doubt. Everybody in there, including myself, had become silent with puzzled looks on our faces. And out of everybody in the shop with their faces balled up, this hoochie only noticed my facial expression.

"Is there a reason yo' face all balled up? Cuz won't nobody talking to yo' ass," she yelled instantly.

Normally I wouldn't respond, but I was boiling at the fact my man was spending large sums of money on that tramp. I stood up, grabbed my things, and headed toward the door, but before leaving I made one statement.

"If you must know why I had such an expression on my face, it's because Snake is *my* man, and I can't believe he would spend *our* money on a tramp like *you*." I darted out the door as fast as I could and headed for my car.

"Thank God I parked close," I said softly as I pressed the keychain to unlock the door.

Pop!

A striking pain flowed through my head. Unfortunately, I didn't get to the car fast enough. That hussy had hit me in the head with her hooker heels.

"You talkin' all that shit, bitch. Now back dat shit up!" she yelled while pulling me by my hair.

I turned around slowly as I struggled to gain my balance and focus.

"Get the fuck off me, you beast!" I yelled as I struggled to free myself from the grips of the monster.

It was like a circus around me. People were circled around us, screaming and yelling, "Fight! Fight! Beat her ass! Ooohhh! She knock the shit outta her!"

I looked around quickly for an escape. Toward the shop, all I could see were women watching from the salon window. To my right was a female spectator with hanging tracks, and even a girl with a head full of relaxer. Out of all these people, I had not one person as a savior, so as a final strand of hope for survival, I opened the Mace on my keychain and emptied the can in her face. I could feel her grip on my hair loosen immediately. Once I realized I was free, I used that as an opportunity to talk shit and possibly redeem myself.

"Take that, bitch. That will teach your ass to stay away from my man!"

As the stripper ran for cover, I jumped in my car and drove off. I noticed my hair was wet and sticking to my neck. I found that odd because I don't usually sweat. When I reached back to lift my hair off my neck, my hand was covered in blood. I rushed to the nearest hospital in a panic. When I got out of the car, there was blood all over the headrest. My head began to feel light as I walked in the emergency room.

Two hours and three stitches later, I was all patched up and headed home. To my surprise, Snake was there when I arrived. He sat on the couch with his feet propped up on the coffee table in a wife-beater, jeans, and Tims, talking on his cell with one hand and massaging his penis with the other. He didn't even notice my presence as he chatted away.

"You better stop talking like that, girl, before I come over there and do something to you."

I walked right up behind him without saying a word and smacked the taste out his mouth. As a reaction, he reached for his gun and jumped up, ready to fire.

"Oh, you're gonna shoot me now, Snake?" My eyes filled with tears. I knew he wasn't going to shoot me, but all the events of the day had taken a toll, and I couldn't take it any longer.

"What the fuck you smack me for, Danielle?" he asked as he placed his gun on the table and walked toward me.

I began to yell and punch him continuously across his chest. "I hate you, Snake. I hate you. Look at me. This is all because you can't keep your ass out of the damn strip club."

Snake's eyes filled with anger as he examined my head. "What the fuck happened, Danielle? Who did this shit?"

"One of your stripper bitches."

"Who? What's her name? What she look like? Where did you see her?" He ran off question after question. Unfortunately, I didn't have many answers.

"Look, I don't know the bitch's name. I ran into her at Creative Styles this morning. She's brown skin, about five-five, small waist, big ass, and long blonde weave. You should know. Evidently you gave her a pretty good amount of money last night. How did you do that, Snake? You were in two places at once? I thought you were pulling an all-nighter!" I replied angrily.

I walked up the stairs to take a shower and wash my hair. I left him standing in the living room, yelling alone. I knew Snake was spending time at the strip club. Hell, I even followed him a couple of times, but I had no idea it was this serious. I tried to convince myself that it didn't matter as long as he came home to me. Now I saw it did matter, and I was going to have to put my foot down.

As the days passed, Snake continued his regular routine, so again I decided to follow him. He made a few stops in Park Place then headed to the strip club, just as I figured. I prepared myself for a two-hour wait as he entered the club. This time I decided to stay until he left and see if he went home or elsewhere. Not even two minutes passed when Snake came back out. Following him was a nice-looking female with a nice body. She wore designer labels from head to toe. I knew Snake was responsible for her appearance. Hell, it was almost identical to mine!

They got in his truck and pulled out of the parking lot. I was careful not to follow them too closely as they crept down the interstate. Snake headed toward the oceanfront. I knew there could only be one destination—Crown Grand Suites. That was Snake's spot for every occasion. I didn't even bother to follow any farther. If they were headed to the hotel, there was only one thing they could be doing. Besides, if I did catch him, what would I do or say? And I definitely wasn't risking getting my ass whipped again.

I got off the exit and returned home. I decided to call Snake on the way.

"What's up, baby girl?" he said as though he wasn't even with a female.

I wanted to cuss him out and tell him how much I hated him for cheating, but instead I played along.

"Nothing, baby. Where are you?" I asked.

"It's not past my curfew yet, is it?" he said, laughing.

I was not amused at all.

"Whatever, Snake. Imagine that—you with a curfew. Can you answer my question, please?"

He was intentionally stalling.

"I think you already know," he responded, still avoiding the question.

"Snake! Where are you?" I said very firmly.

"I'm on my way to this bachelor party. I had to pick up the stripper for my man. I'll be at the oceanfront. You know my spot," he said calmly.

I had overreacted. I was glad I did turn around instead of making a scene.

CHAPTER 9

A FRIEND'S DECEIT

BJ

"Aaaaahhh!" I screamed as Duke forced his penis inside of me.

Luckily, no one was home to hear my screams, but as loud as I was, I was more concerned with the neighbors hearing me at this point.

"Please take it slow, Duke," I begged with every pump he gave. I had no idea losing my virginity would hurt so badly.

"Okay . . . I got you. Just work with me, BJ. Let me get it all the way in first."

I wrapped my arms around him tightly as he slid his hands under my butt cheeks and pushed me forward, giving one big thrush.

"Ooohhh shiiiiit!" I yelled out in pain.

It felt like my insides were ripping in half. Duke began to kiss my neck softly while caressing my breasts. His gentle touch made things feel a lot better. I could feel the pain turn into pleasure. I moved my pelvis slowly in tune with his movements. My vagina became moist, making our sex even more enjoyable. I ran my fingers through Duke's hair as he sexed me. I began to moan with pleasure instead of pain.

"You like that?" Duke whispered in my ear as he kissed my neck.

He made me feel so good inside. The truth was, I did like it, and now I understand why Gina wanted so much as well.

"Yes," I moaned softly as he continuously sexed me until he busted a nut.

After sex, Duke sparked a blunt as I lay next to

him in bed. I couldn't believe I had finally lost my virginity. Too bad I couldn't share it with Gina. I had betrayed my best friend for a guy. I broke a pact that we promised to never break. We always said we would never let a guy come between us. I felt really bad, like I had just made a huge mistake.

"Duke. What have we done?" I asked him with a pitiful look on my face.

"What'chu mean?" he asked.

I tried to explain. "You're sexing Gina, and she's my best friend. I have totally violated. I have crossed boundaries I should have never come near."

"Whateva, BJ. You been coming at me ever since the day you caught me and Gina fucking."

Duke upset me with that comment; as if he never returned the flirt or something. In fact, we wouldn't be together right now if he hadn't done that shiesty shit at Gina's house. I decided to throw that in his face.

"If I'm not mistaken, you were the one eating my coochie in Gina's living room while she was upstairs with Ray-Ray."

"You wanted it, BJ. That's why you ratted her out. But if you feel so guilty, let's just end it here and forget it ever happened."

He put out his blunt and threw on his clothes. I wished we didn't have to end it like that, but I was happy with the decision. I would hate to lose Gina as a friend.

I stopped him as he headed to the door. "Bye, Duke." I looked at him with my best puppy dog eyes before kissing him on the lips.

CHUNICHI

He hugged me tight. "I'll see you 'round, shortie."

I knew I was making the right decision, but my heart was broken as I watched him leave through the window.

Ring . . . ring.

The caller ID read: REGINA WALLACE.

It was Gina. She must have felt me being deceitful.

"What's up, girl?" I answered in a fake, tone.

"Nothing. I was just calling to see what's up. You coming over today?"

Normally I would be at Gina's house at least five times a week, but since I had been dealing with Duke, I felt too guilty to come around.

"Nah, girl. I'm home alone, so I'm going to chill. But me and Ray-Ray will come over tomorrow," I lied.

As the weeks passed, I didn't sex Duke or even speak to him. Gina, on the other hand, was sexing him on the regular. In fact, she was sexing both Ray-Ray and Duke.

Valentine's Day was right around the corner, and I hated the thought of being alone. For once, the tables had turned, and *I* was now envious of *Gina*. Even though I was jealous of all the attention she had been receiving from Ray-Ray and Duke, I still kept my promise and stayed away from Duke. It was hard, though. Each time I saw him, my heart would flutter, but I always kept my distance.

Valentine's Day rolled around sooner than I

expected. Gina had all sorts of plans and needed my assistance to make sure everything went accordingly. After Duke and Ray-Ray ran into each other at Gina's house, they were each under the impression that Gina had dropped the other. Gina patched that situation up real quick. Since then, things were lovely for her. She had all the newest shoes and clothes times two. Between the gifts from the two of them, Gina stayed laced.

She planned to spend the first part of the day with Duke then go out later that night with Ray-Ray. It was my job to keep Ray-Ray occupied until then. She called me about noon.

"Hey, girl. I just wanted to make sure we had the plans together."

I was hoping she would have been calling to tell me Duke stood her up, but I wasn't that lucky.

"Yeah, I got you. Keep Ray-Ray busy until you call, right? If you don't call, just let him come around seven," I said in an unconcerned voice.

We had gone over the plan a thousand times. I didn't see the need of her calling and giving me the run-down for the thousandth-and-one time.

"Come on, girl. What you doing in there?" I could hear Duke banging on the door, yelling in the background.

"Where are you?" I asked, eager to know what Duke had planned for her.

"I'm at the oceanfront at the Crown Grand Suites. The room is beautiful, and the sight is gorgeous. We've been here all day. We plan to watch the sunset on the ocean and everything, girl. My day has been great so far. But I got to go. He's rushing me. Just listen out for my call."

I hung up the phone without saying a word. I cried myself to sleep as I could only dream about being in her shoes.

I woke to the annoying buzz of my alarm clock later that day. It was six-thirty and time for me to call Ray-Ray.

"Yo? What's up, li'l cuz?" he asked.

"Come on, it's time to meet up with Gina," I said sleepily.

"I'm on my way," he said before hanging up.

Ten minutes later he was at my house. I ran downstairs and jumped in the car. We flew down Martin Luther King Boulevard toward Curry Village, where Gina lived. We pulled up near her house and headed for the door. I knocked on the door as Ray-Ray stood beside me with a teddy, flowers, balloons, and all sorts of bags in his hands. He didn't want Gina to see what he had for her, so he hid so she couldn't see him through the peephole.

"Hey, girl," she said as she opened the door.

I didn't respond. I just smiled and stepped aside so Ray–Ray could appear with his surprise. Ray-Ray walked in and hugged her.

"Happy Val—" He stopped in the middle of his sentence and dropped everything.

I stood at the door behind him, wondering what was going on. All of a sudden I saw him rush forward and Gina screamed. I walked in the room and Ray-Ray and Duke were locked up together, tousling. Gina and I tried our hardest to pull them apart.

"Please stop it. Please!" I begged Ray-Ray. Eventually, we were able to pull them apart.

"Get my shit from that bitch, BJ," Ray-Ray said as he headed to his car.

I grabbed the bags, leaving the torn flowers, balloons, and teddy behind. I didn't know what to do, so I just did what he asked and decided to call Gina later. I ran out the door and jumped in the car. Three minutes didn't pass before Gina was calling Ray-Ray's phone. He didn't even bother to answer. He was heated, and didn't have anything to say to her. She eventually stopped calling, but she did leave a message. He checked his voicemail as we rode around. Ray-Ray decided to ride and smoke to clear his mind. He handed me the phone after listening to the message.

"Call your girl. She trippin', yo."

I wondered what she said on the voicemail. I called her right away. The phone rang one time and she picked up.

"You shiesty, bitch! When I see you I'm going to fuck yo' ass up," she yelled into the phone.

I had no idea what she was talking about. I figured she was upset that I took the things, so I tried to explain. "What are you talking about, Gina? Ray-Ray asked me to get the gifts. I only grabbed them because there was enough tension already. I didn't want to make things worse. Girl, you know I would have brought them back over there later." I tried to make things a little smoother.

"Bitch, I don't give a fuck about no clothes. I'm talking about how you set me up. I specifically told

70

you not to bring him if I call. I called a thousand times and you didn't answer. I even left five messages on your voicemail. We went through this a thousand times. I knew you were going to do some shit because you're jealous of me. You hate the fact that I'm on top for once and I have all the attention, and not BJ. I've been noticing little shit for the past month. I see how you look at Duke and wear little clothes around him, and say slick shit out your mouth. I just chose to trust you because you were my girl. I thought we would never let a guy come between us, but I guess that was bullshit too."

I couldn't believe Gina. She actually thought I had set her up. I was angry, but more hurt than anything. I had no idea she thought such bad things of me. I decided to make one last desperate attempt to repair our friendship.

"Gina, I swear on everything I have, I didn't set you up. I was sleeping all day. When my alarm went off I jumped up and called Ray-Ray. I didn't even check my voicemail."

"Yeah, I figured that's what you would say. But don't worry about it. I owe you, bitch." Those were the last words she spoke before hanging up in my ear.

Weeks passed and I didn't hear from or see Gina. I really missed her, but my pride wouldn't let me bow down. I constantly reminded myself I did my part. I tried to resolve the issue, but she wasn't trying to hear it. Each day at school, I was reminded of the situation. There was steady gossip about me setting Gina up. There were even a few times the word out was I was supposed to get jumped by Gina and her crew from out the way. Nevertheless, I still remained me. I still went to school each day, I still sat in the same spot at lunch and I still walked the same halls. Gina knew me better than anyone, and she knew it would definitely take an army to beat me. I would pick up a weapon, fight dirty, or even avoid a fight if I was outnumbered, but I would never lose. No one would ever have the honor of saying they beat my ass.

I thought the day would never come, but Gina and I finally met face-to-face. After school one Friday, I was leaving the building. As I walked to the bus, I noticed Duke. I figured since Gina and I were no longer friends and now she was all about Ray-Ray, I may as well rekindle my relations with Duke.

"Can I roll with you?" I asked in my most seductive tone.

Duke paused and examined me from head to toe. Luckily, I had on stretch jeans and a baby tee, so he could see my figure perfectly. He hugged me with a pleasing look on his face.

"You been keeping my shit tight?" he asked as he squeezed my bottom.

"Sure have," I gladly boasted.

"Well, that's all I need to hear. Come on, I'm parked over here." Duke pointed to a black Lexus GS 400.

He always kept nice cars, but I was really

impressed with this one. I got in the car with no hesitation. Just as Duke began to pull off, a hoop-ride steered in front of us, cutting him off.

"Damn. What the fuck does this bitch want?" Duke mumbled under his breath.

I looked up and it was Gina. She jumped out of the car and headed to my side. Before I could register what was going on, she reached in the window and stole me right in the face. As a reaction, I grabbed her shirt, pulling her toward the inside of the car. I reached in my pocket with my free hand and pulled out my shank. I always kept it near for situations such as this. Within seconds, my shank was out and Gina had been stabbed three times in the chest area. Afraid that his car would get damaged, Duke quickly ran over and broke things up. I looked in the mirror to examine my face as Gina returned to her hoop-ride. I wiped the trickle of blood that dripped from my right nostril. Duke looked at me, examining my face as well.

"You a'ight?" he asked sincerely.

"Yeah, I'm fine. Where we headed?" I quickly changed the subject, eager to put the whole thing behind me.

"Wherever you want to go, sweetheart. You missed me?" Duke asked while rubbing my inner thigh. I smiled and nodded. He looked so damn good driving his Lex with the Clipse banging in the background.

"Those niggas couldn't have said it any better. Virginia's for hustlers." He quoted the infamous words of the Clipse.

MARRIED TO THE GAME

I wondered how the fuck would he know. He'd been living off his uncle since I'd known him. I questioned him to see if things had changed.

"How would you know, Duke? You ain't never sold shit."

"Yeah, that's what you and the rest of these niggas out here think. But that's cool. I like it like that. It keeps my name clear. I ain't gotta prove shit to nobody, ma."

I could tell he was getting offended, so I switched things up to turn the conversation around.

"You got something to prove to me," I said while untying his du-rag so that I could play in his cornrows.

"Oh yeah? And what's that?"

"That you can't be whipped."

He thought that statement was very funny. "You got a long way to go, young buck. You can't even say the word whipped until you start fucking for real."

He was right. I couldn't get him whipped just yet, because I just got started, but little did he know it wouldn't be long. I felt like I was a natural. My body moved without hesitation. Once I got to the point that I could stand the pain, I was going to be a beast in bed, and Duke would be the first to know.

CHAPTER 10

MY BABY DADDY

GINA

"Shit!" I yelled as I checked the pregnancy test. I couldn't believe my eyes. I knew that having unprotected sex could result in an unwanted pregnancy, but I guess I just never thought it could happen to someone like me.

It had been days since the fight with BJ, but the stab wounds I received while fighting with her still hadn't quite healed. The streaking pain I felt with each motion was a constant reminder of the revenge I owed her. I hadn't come up with the perfect plan, but I was definitely going to get her back. Now that I realized she could've made me lose my unborn child, I was furious.

The only real thing that was keeping me off BJ's ass was her cousin. If I didn't love Ray-Ray so much, I would have sent bitches to her house that same day. But mark my word—her day would come. Even if it took me months to get her, I knew my revenge on BJ was coming. At the moment, I had more important things to worry about, like the fact that my period hadn't come in a month, and that I was sitting staring at a colored cotton tip of an exposed pregnancy test.

I was in a sad state of denial, so I reached under the bathroom counter to retrieve the extra test I'd purchased. I slowly removed the wrapper and sat on the toilet, placing the open end of the test-tube under the flow of my urine. Once it was soaked, I replaced the cap.

Now the waiting game, I thought as I set the test on the bathroom counter and went to watch a little TV. I hoped Dave Chappelle's antics would make the time pass, but my stomach ached with fear as I waited the minutes that seemed to take hours. I reflected on the first test and thought that perhaps there had been a defect in it. After all, most of those over-the-counter pregnancy tests were only ninety-nine percent positive.

Two commercials later, the time was up, and I hesitantly returned to the bathroom. I almost hit the floor when I saw that plus sign in bright pink.

Oh, shit, then it must be true. I'm pregnant! I nearly broke my neck as I rushed through the house, jumping over chairs and running up the stairs to get my phone to call Ray-Ray.

"Happy birthday, baby!" Ray-Ray yelled into the phone as soon as he picked up.

Although his greeting was a beautiful notion, I had a tough time accepting it at the moment.

"Fuck a birthday!" I yelled. "You and me got some issues."

"Damn, what's up with you? I guess that's the attitude of a black birthday girl, huh?" Ray-Ray said in an attempt to ease the tension.

"Nah, this is the attitude of a black pregnant birthday girl! This damn pregnancy test is what's up, nigga!" I yelled into the phone.

Since Duke and I were no longer an item, Ray-Ray hadn't been using protection. One night he came over after a long night of gambling and drinking at the bootlegger's, drunk and horny. We engaged in passionate sex and he failed to pull out. I knew I was going to end up pregnant the night it happened, but I hoped for a different outcome.

"What? You pregnant?" he asked with little emotion. "So, what you gonna do?" He continued to speak like the whole ordeal was nothing.

"What am *I* going to do? Did I get pregnant alone, nigga? What are *you* going to do?" I yelled at him.

"Okay, Gina. What are *we* going to do? Ain't no need in all this drama you giving me now," he responded, still with little emotion.

His lack of compassion was really starting to annoy me, so I fought back with words I didn't know I'd come to regret.

"I want an abortion!" I yelled like my mind was bad. I was sure that statement would get his attention, but I ended up with my face cracked, instead. Either Ray-Ray didn't know how to take the hint of a cry for attention, or he just didn't care like I thought he would.

"A'ight. Cool. Just let me know how much it cost. You know I got you," he said before hanging up the phone in my ear.

I sat on my bed, sobbing as I thought about all the recent events in my life.

How did I get in this situation?

Normally, this would be a time when I would call BJ and ask for her support, but not this time. She had betrayed me, and I hated her for it. Duke had betrayed me, and I hated him as well. So had my mother, her boyfriend, and now Ray-Ray too. I had to wonder how one person could be let down so many times. At that moment, it seemed as if I was the only person in the world who had ever been betrayed by just about all the important people in their lives.

How could Ray-Ray have so openly agreed to an abortion? How could he just hang up on me like that without making sure I was okay? Didn't he understand that I loved him? Didn't he know that this child was a part of us both? Tears welled up in my eyes as I continued to think. Maybe this baby was all I got. Maybe this was the only person I could truly trust and love, who would love me the same, no matter the weather.

I sat on my bed weeping until I fell asleep, but my afternoon nap was interrupted by the sound of gunshots. I'd heard gunshots nearby before, but for some reason, these shots seemed eerie. My heart was beating uncontrollably, and I could hardly catch my breath. I looked out the window to see where the shots were coming from, but the neighborhood was as peaceful as an April shower. I figured the shots must have been part of a bad dream, and that being suddenly awakened added to the rapid beat of my heart.

Since I was awake, I decided to call Ray-Ray back and tell him there had been a change of plans. I had decided to keep my baby and there was nothing he could do to stop me. His phone rang, but he didn't answer. I called a few more times after that and someone picked up, but no one said anything. I listened carefully. I heard music in the background and faint breathing. Ray-Ray was listening to our song, "Lovers and Friends" by Lil Jon, Luda, and Usher. For a moment I thought about the countless times we made love to that song, but that moment of reminiscing was cut short when I heard the whisper of someone's voice. I listened attentively. I could hear someone trying to force words out, but I wasn't sure exactly what they were saying. I put my volume up as loud as possible and listened a little harder. And that's when I heard the faint words between gasps of breath, "I . . . I . . . love . . . you . . ."

I dropped the phone on the floor as my brain began to register what had just happened. Immediately, all sorts of images flashed through my head. The worst image of all was my man sexing someone else. I hung up the phone in disbelief. I began sobbing even worse than before.

How could he do this to me? I'm pregnant—and on my birthday!

I was devastated. My tears quickly turned to anger the more I thought about Ray-Ray with someone else. That made it official. I was alone. Everyone I loved had truly betrayed me. There was no longer need for doubt. I decided to call him back as the reality set in. I planned to tell him how he hurt me and how I hated him for it. But this time when I called, the phone went straight to voicemail. He must have discovered the terrible mistake he'd made. I decided to leave a message.

"What's up, this Ray. Leave a message."

Beep!

"Ray-Ray, this is Gina. I'm sure you're busy at the celebrity bash handling your business right now, and that's why your phone is off. But what I have to say needs no conversation anyway. I was just calling to tell you that one, it's over, two, I'm keeping the baby, and three . . . thanks for such a wonderful birthday. And as for as the bitch you're with, I hope she was worth it."

Click!

I hung up the phone confident I had made the right decision. I turned on some music to calm my nerves. But the more I sat, the more the vision of Ray-Ray and another woman stuck in my head. I began to think of who it might be. The first person who came to mind was that conniving bitch BJ. She probably set him up with another chick just to get at me. With that in mind, the anger soon became overwhelming and I could no longer keep my composure.

I jumped up in a panic and threw on my shoes and grabbed my purse. I headed for the door with my mom's car keys in hand, but not before grabbing the gun Ray-Ray kept at my house for backup protection. I was going to find their asses and when I did, it would be a terrible sight. Somebody was gon' die, and I didn't plan for it to be me. I jumped in the car and tried starting it up. Tears welled up in my eyes once again, as I struggled to get the car started.

"Come on, you stupid car!" I yelled hysterically.

I tried and tried turning the ignition, but nothing—not a sound. Not even a stutter. The car wouldn't start. Frustrated and exhausted, I just sat in the car and cried. I lit a blunt as I often did in situations that were stressful, in an attempt to relieve some tension. After about ten minutes of sobbing and smoking, I actually felt a little better. I got myself together, got out of the car, and headed back to the house. Once in my bedroom I undressed and lay down. I didn't even bother calling Ray-Ray's sorry ass again. Within moments, the tension lifted from my body and I was sound asleep.

CHAPTER 11

BEEF ON THE STREETS

SNAKE

Shit was really starting to get hectic around here. These stripping bitches were getting out of control. Ceazia's pussy was getting better by the day, my girl was going mad, my little nigga, Duke, had beef, and I thought I might have picked up a little personal beef of my own.

After that trick at the beauty salon busted my girl in the head, I went ballistic. I went up to that shop and threatened to shut the shit down unless somebody told me what the fuck happened that day. Of course, it didn't take long for them to start squealing. I walked in calmly with my gun in hand and locked the door behind me. I stood at the door and asked DeeDee what was up. She didn't have much to say, so I asked the assistant. She didn't have much to say, either. So, in order to get the information I needed, I had to start making threats. I didn't want to do that because DeeDee is my man's old lady, but shit, my girl was involved and I had to do what I had to do. After the threats, those bitches started singing. I found out it was a trick that goes by the name of Cherry at one of the local strip joints. I paid her a visit that same night. As soon as I hit the door, it was as though an alarm had been hit, 'cause every bitch in there came running from the back.

"Nah, baby, I ain't here for that tonight." I dissed one of my regular chicks I would normally holla at.

She'd approached me with the usual enticement. Normally, this would have caught my attention, but not tonight. I was on a mission and I had no time for chatting, flirting, or any bullshit. It didn't take long for me to spot Cherry in a dark corner turning her normal tricks. I walked right up behind her tricking ass and grabbed that bitch by her weave.

"Aaaahh! What the fuck is going on?" she squealed as I dragged her from the gentlemen she was entertaining and into the men's bathroom.

"Bitch, you done lost your muthafucking mind?" I asked while choking Cherry against the bathroom wall.

"I'm sorry, baby. I ain't know that was your girl." She began to beg off the jump.

That grimy bitch already knew she'd fucked up.

"Bitch . . . don't . . . you ever . . . come near my girl or anybody that got anything to do with me again." I said while smacking her between words.

"Okay, okay. Please just don't hit me anymore, Snake, please. Whatever you want, baby, please." She continued to beg.

By this time, security was rushing the bathroom. "Yo, what the fuck is going on?" I could hear one security guard yell.

I turned around so he could get a look at my face. I figured he must didn't know who I was to rush in talking shit like that.

"Oh, Snake. You a'ight?" he asked in a totally different tone.

"Yeah, I'm straight," I said then directed my attention back to Cherry, who was now standing up confidently.

"Bitch, this ain't over," I said to her then

pushed her in the face.

I straightened my clothes then walked out of the men's restroom calmly. I stopped at the bar, drank a shot of Patron then exited the club. As I rode home, I was confident that the next time Cherry saw Danielle, her attitude would be a lot better.

Now that the situation was dealt with, I began to think about my li'l soldier, Duke. It seemed like he's caught beef behind some little hot-ass female. I had to school him on that shit. It was getting harder and harder to school that li'l nigga these days. Seemed like I noticed a change in him every day.

My brain jumped from one issue to another. As if my issue with Cherry and Duke wasn't enough, now Danielle had been tripping too. I didn't know what was up with her. Seemed like she was changing daily, just like Duke. All I could say was, "Thank God my game is tight." She'd been following me, checking my text messages and phone, and even searching through my pockets. I didn't make a fuss, though. I just played along and watched my steps. She was starting to scare me. I was not trying to end up like my brother, Vegas.

The other night, I went to the strip club to pick up Ceazia, and Danielle was following me. I didn't realize she was following me until I was on the interstate and almost to the oceanfront. Now, the average nigga would have panicked, but instead, I started to plot. I knew Danielle didn't know what Ceazia looked like, so that wasn't a worry. But she did know where my spot was on the oceanfront.

She knew I would be headed to one place, the Crown Grand Suites. Five minutes from the destination, I received a phone call from her. I played it cool, and the lies just rolled off my tongue. I came off on top. Danielle's whole attitude switched. Instead of me being the bad one, she felt guilty for accusing me.

Now, let's chat about Ceazia. That bitch was venomous. I knew it before I even fucked her, but she was so irresistible. It was taking all I could to stay away, but she kept reeling me in. I was about to switch it up on her to keep me in the safe zone.

Ring, ring . . .

I knew it wouldn't be long before Ceazia called. That gave me the perfect opportunity to switch up on her.

"Yo!"

"What's up, baby? Are we meeting up tonight at the usual spot?" she asked in her signature sexy voice.

As bad as I wanted to get with her, I knew I couldn't, but by the same token, I had to lead her on. I wanted to back off, but I needed to keep her on the offense at the same time. That way she would be constantly trying to get at me.

"Yeah, I'll hit you up around ten. Keep your phone on."

"Okay," she readily agreed.

"A'ight, sweetheart. I'll talk to you later." I hung up and headed out the way to holla at Duke.

We had a full weekend ahead of us. It was the Annual Seven Cities Celebrity Weekend Bash. All the hottest entertainers, athletes, and ballers were sure to attend. Everyone looked forward to this event each year. It was the time for us to shine.

"What up, Unc?" Duke said as he hopped in the truck.

"What's up with you, nigga? Word on the street is you got beef. Care to fill me in on that shit?"

"Oh really, 'cause word on the street is you're in that same boat," Duke snapped back.

I hated when Duke got sarcastic. He was growing up fast, and the fear I used to put in his heart was no longer there. I was beginning to see at some point he was going to challenge me. And each incident like this just confirmed that day was getting closer.

"I can handle my shit, young buck. Can you say the same?" I said while punching him in the chest as a reminder that I was still the boss.

"Man, that ain't no beef for real. That nigga, Ray-Ray, is just a little upset about a little tousle we had at Gina's crib on Valentines Day. That is old."

"Ray-Ray? Ain't you knocking his little cousin off?"

Duke was really getting himself in a fucked up position. He didn't know when that nigga might pop up. Ray-Ray could be around when he was going to scoop shortie or anything. I tried to explain the danger of what he was doing.

"Man, I'm good. I got this shit together."

Needless to say, his head was big, and I couldn't tell him nothing. I ended the conversation there.

"A'ight, Li'l Soldier. Handle your handle," I said

as we pulled up to the Quick Shop on the corner.

I ran in the store to buy a box of blunts. I could see the chickens flocking around the truck, trying to holla at Duke.

I gotta teach that nigga to have a low profile, I thought. I was sure we had already been over that shit, but I guess it didn't sink in. By the time I arrived back to the truck, Duke was standing outside the door, hugging on some hood-rat chick.

"Yo, Duke. Come on, nigga."

"A'ight, mami," Duke said to the chick as he smacked her ass before hopping in the truck.

"A'ight, young fuck," she said, winking.

That nigga had absolutely no standards. I had to straighten him on that shit immediately!

"Duke! What the fuck you doing, man? You just can't be knocking any old bitch off. You gotta make it a privilege to fuck. Otherwise, the top-notch bitches not gonna be trying to fuck."

"Man, that's an old head. How many niggas my age hitting old heads? Why you think she calls me her young fuck? I don't give a damn about these young chicks no more, man. I got some shit in store. I'm 'bout to knock off a couple of real bomb-ass top-notch bitches."

I was afraid to even inquire. That nigga, Duke, was really feeling himself. Who knew what he was planning to do?

Thirty minutes later, we were at the Hampton Coliseum. We pulled up and parked front and center. I knew niggas wouldn't be ready for my truck. It's events like these I looked forward to. Niggas was dizzy by the spin of the 24-inch Stop and Go's on the Range. I copped it especially for this event. Me and Duke hopped out the truck to holla at a few people.

"What up, Snake?" Martinez was the first to greet me. He had an odd look on his face.

"What's good, man?" I returned the greeting.

"Not too much, man. It's a lot of envy out here today. As matter of fact, I've heard whispers of your name."

I knew something was up. I know that nigga, Martinez, like the back of my hand.

"Oh yeah. What they talking?"

"It's that nigga Joker. Talking about he gotta straighten you 'bout running up in his girl's spot."

I knew it had to be that. I pretty much stayed low on the streets, so I rarely had beef. I wasn't concerned at all.

"That's it, man? That's what got you worried, nigga? Where dat nigga at?"

"That ain't it, man. I know you can handle yours. It's more to it."

Now this nigga was *really* starting to piss me off.

"What is it, nigga?" I was aggravated by his hesitation.

"It's Duke, man. Nigga's talking about getting that nigga."

I understood why Martinez hesitated with that statement. When it comes to my little soldier, I don't fuck around.

"Oh yeah . . . . Who the fuck is talking?" My eyes burned with fury.

"It's that nigga, Ray-Ray."

Me and Duke just had that conversation. Now was the time for me to really talk with him.

"Duke." I called him over as I contemplated on leaving the game.

Do I coach him on defense or do I just send him home?

Duke was a hothead, and I was afraid how he may react. I didn't want anything to happen to him, and I didn't want him to do anything he would regret. I had to make a decision and fast.

"What's the deal, Unc? You fucking with my game right now." Duke was more concerned with hollering at the ladies than his own safety.

"Duke, on some real shit, I gotta holla at you."

We headed back to the truck and jumped in. I looked Duke in the eyes.

"Tell me what's up with you and this nigga Ray-Ray."

Duke came back with an explosive laugh. "Unc. Please tell me you ain't got me in here about that nigga."

Just like I figured, this nigga had no idea. I started the truck.

"What you doing, Snake? We just got here, man. I know you ain't gon' let this fool punk us."

I had nothing to prove to Duke, so I didn't respond. I just put the truck in reverse.

"Stop the muthafucking truck, man!" Duke demanded.

"Who the fuck you hollering at, nigga?" I asked just as forcefully.

Duke didn't respond. He just stared at me with a killer grit.

"Fix yo' face," I said while grabbing him by the collar, trying once again to instill the fear that seemed no longer present in Duke's heart.

I got a surprising reply.

"Fuck you! I ain't no damn child no more, Snake!" he yelled while forcefully pushing me in the chest.

My first instinct was to punch this li'l nigga in his face and break his fucking jaw, but instead I chose to let him learn the hard way.

Ssskuuuurrrrt!

I slammed on breaks almost giving both of us whiplash.

"You think you hard, nigga? Then get the fuck out. Hold ya own!" I handed him the nine from my waist.

Duke jumped out of the truck with no hesitation.

"Oh, and I got my own to handle my own," he said as he handed me the gun, pulled out a chrome nine of his own and cocked it back before replacing it on his waist.

As soon as he jumped out, I pulled off.

Just as I was headed out of the parking lot, I ran into Ceazia. She was looking fly as shit, too. I pulled up behind her BMW. She was the only female at the Coliseum killing the scene with the white 745 LI with the chromed factories, newborn with the paper tags and straight glasshouse, no tent. She was definitely doing the damn thang.

"What's up, baby girl?" I asked as I stroked her underneath the chin.

She grinned and looked at me seductively with

those panther eyes. "You," she simply responded before lightly kissing my lips.

I could feel my nature rising. I didn't know what it was about that chick, but she had a deadly trance. Vegas always used to mention the crazy things she would do. He used to say it was voodoo. He believed every now and then, she would pull something from her Haitian roots. And now I was starting to believe the same shit.

"I see you killing them with the Range and spinners. How can I get down? You got some spinners for me?" she asked while checking out my truck.

I laughed. She and I both knew exactly what it would take for her to get down.

"You know what it takes. What's good for tonight?" I asked while checking out her body in those stretch Lady Evisus.

"I don't know. You got something . . .?"

Bang! Bang! Bang! Bang!

Our conversation was interrupted by gunshots.

"Get in the truck!" I yelled.

Ceazia jumped in the back seat behind me. I pulled off immediately, glancing in my rearview mirror. Shit was chaotic; people were running in every direction.

Bang! Bang! Bang! Bang!

The gunshots were neverending. I glanced in the rearview mirror once again. I was not prepared for the image before me.

Ssskuuuurrrrt!

I slammed on brakes then busted a U-turn in the middle of the parking lot and headed back to the scene. Once there, I jumped out of the truck, my heart pounding, people running, and cars pulling off in every direction. It was as though none of these things existed as I ran closer to the center of the action. Everything around me moved slowly the closer I got. I could hear Ceazia screaming in the background.

"Snaaaake, noooooo!"

I could feel Martinez pulling my arm as I grabbed my nine from my waist, but his grip wasn't strong enough to hold back the aggression flowing through my veins. As I took my final steps, my body froze with disbelief. It was my li'l soldier, dying on the battlefield, but still holding his gun at attention. I was so taken by the scene before me I didn't realize Ray-Ray was standing in front of me with his gun pointed at Duke. My brain raced as we looked eye-to-eye—never saying a word.

Do I get him before he gets me? Or if I threaten to get him, will he get Duke?

I decided to take my chances. I quickly aimed my gun, but Ray-Ray beat me to the punch.

Click . . . click . . . click.

Saved by the bell! That bitch nigga was out of bullets. Left with no other choice, he jumped in his car in a desperate attempt to escape. I took my time aiming at him, confident he wouldn't get far.

Shots rang out for the final time. I was puzzled by the sounds I heard as Ray-Ray's body jumped and bounced with every bullet as if he was having convulsions. When the shooting ceased, his body lay slumped over into the passenger's seat of his car. I glanced around quickly as I grabbed Duke and put him in the truck, but I saw no one. There was only me, Duke, and Ray-Ray, struggling to reload his gun in his car. I sped off.

"That fool ain't gon' make it. Let him die slowly," were my final words as I headed to the nearest hospital.

We rode in silence as I sped through every red light on the way. I glanced down and noticed my blood-soaked sleeve. I'd been hit in my right arm. My brain raced as I tried to figure out where the shots came from.

Maybe those final shots were meant for me. The ones fired before I even had a chance to pull the trigger on my gun. I looked around to see who may have fired the shots, but saw no one.

I was just glad me and Duke were still here, because I'd fucked up. This shit would have never gone down if I'd gone with my first instinct and just left the Coliseum, forcing Duke to come along.

CHAPTER 12

WATCH YA BACK

CHUNICHI

UNKNOWN MAN

Always lurking, again I was on the scene. I'd heard of the beef Duke and Snake both carried on the streets, and I knew this would be the event where shit would go down. That's why I made sure I was there. There was no way I was going to let them niggas die at the hands of anyone else. This was my revenge, and I would be the one to lay them to rest.

Young niggas these days were trying to get on the map, and they were willing to do anything to earn a name. They would rob, shoot, and kill, just to be the man on the block with the most respect. Duke already had respect because of his family, which put him in a dangerous position. Any nigga that wanted to rise up could knock him off and get automatic respect on the streets. And that's exactly why I had a team of young cats by my side— trained to kill. All I had to do was give 'em the word. Today was a small test of just how quick one of my li'l dudes could be on the trigga.

I would pay a million dollars to have an instant replay of the look on Snake's face when he heard the shots ring out. He looked as though his life had flashed before his eyes. It's sad I had to take that li'l nigga Ray-Ray down, but somebody had to go. If I had not put him down then Snake or Duke, if not both of them, would surely be gone. And I couldn't have him throw a wrench in my plan. I have something special planned for them.

Funny how life works, huh? Snake and Duke were two niggas that I wanted dead, and because of me, they were alive. Looked like their beef was just about to catch up with them, but because I stepped in, they'd been given another day in this grimy-ass place.

Snake was caught slipping again. He should have never left Duke at that celebrity event alone. Duke had better be thankful that gold-digging bitch, C, was there to keep Snake around for a little while longer. If not, he would have been nowhere in sight when Duke got hit. I was sure this day would definitely be used to Ceazia's advantage. She could turn any situation into a position that worked in her favor.

CHAPTER 13

CHAOTIC CRISIS

CEAZIA

Snake's phone rang continuously while en route to the hospital. Everyone was anxious to know what was going on. I noticed that out of all the hundred and one calls he'd received, he ignored them all except one. From the way the conversation went, I was sure he was speaking with his girl.

"Baby, shit is crazy. I'm on my way to the hospital . . . I'm a'ight, but Duke was shot . . . . I'm leaving Hampton and on my way to Norfolk General," Snake ranted into the phone.

Snake answered question after question as though he was being interrogated. I rolled my eyes out of jealousy then quickly focused my attention back to Duke. I held him tightly as blood drained from his nose and mouth.

"Hold on, Li'l Soldier, you're gonna make it, baby," I reassured him as I tried to fight the images that constantly flashed in my head.

All I could envision was Vegas lying in the Jacuzzi filled with his own blood. I could picture the two women lying doubled-over in the Jacuzzi— dead along with Vegas. The thought was clear as if it was just the day before, when I unloaded my gun on them.

It seemed like only moments had passed once we got to the hospital because it wasn't long before we pulled up to the emergency room. Snake rushed to the back and pulled Duke out the back door. Others rushed over to help him. It didn't take long for them to get Duke in the hospital and for the emergency team to come and roll him off to the trauma unit. Family members and friends arrived at the hospital shortly after we did. Everyone was hysterical.

"Who did this? Where was he shot? Is he going to make it? How is he?" Everyone questioned Snake at once.

I could see the frustration and tension in Snake's face. He didn't respond to anyone. He just stood in the middle of the floor, motionless. I'd never seen him speechless and so full of anguish over anything. I knew he was going to explode at any moment.

"Why don't we go outside and get some air?" I suggested, while taking his hand, leading him toward the exit.

Surprisingly, he followed along without argument. Once outside, he sat on the bench, rubbing his head. Stress was written all over his face. Duke was his li'l soldier, and they were extremely close. I could understand why he was so upset about his li'l homey being shot. Snake finally spoke, blaming himself for not having Duke's back in time.

"I shouldn't have left him there alone. I could have prevented this shit," he said as tears rolled from his eyes.

I never thought I would see the day Snake would shed a tear. This moment called for immediate attention. I placed my arm around his shoulder and offered words of comfort.

"It's not your fault, Snake. There is nothing you could have done. He's going to be fine." I hugged him tightly.

Snake tensed up as I hugged him. I pulled back and examined him. His sleeve was red in color, when it wasn't supposed to be.

"It's my arm. I'm hit," he said calmly. "I've been so distraught over my li'l soldier that I didn't realize I'd been hit too."

Noticing that his sleeve was soaked in blood, I panicked and immediately jumped up to get help. I asked Snake to remain where he was until I came back with a nurse. Snake grabbed my arm, preventing me from moving.

"Please, I don't want any help right now. I just need a minute to think," he pleaded.

"Okay, Snake, but you're going to eventually need to get that looked at."

I agreed to give him a few moments before getting him medical attention. Drops of blood soon began hitting the ground, but Snake still refused to get help at the moment. His mind was heavy in thought, so I respected his wishes of solitude. He did, however, okay me to stay with him.

We didn't say any words to each other. We just sat in the cool night air, embracing one another. I watched as people constantly walked in and out of the emergency room waiting area. I noticed a nice-looking young lady walking briskly toward us. She had a perfect frame and flawless skin. Her designer attire was definitely an outfit that would fit into the closet of a diva like me. As she walked closer, she examined me closely, eventually pausing directly before me.

"My name is Danielle. I'm Snake's girlfriend.

And you are?" she said as she extended her hand.

I felt embarrassed as I extended my bloody hand. My hair was a mess and I had blood all over my clothes.

"Hi. I'm—"

"You're a stripper," she interrupted me.

Out of respect for Snake, I didn't respond. That bitch had no idea who I was. Normally, I would have whipped her ass just for walking up on me the way she did.

"Danielle . . . now is not the time for this shit," Snake interjected.

I was glad he responded before I did. She looked me up and down, examining every inch of my body.

"From the looks of things, you were around when all this took place. And what exactly were you doing with my man, if I may ask?"

"Look, Danielle, I am Vegas—"

"You don't have to explain," Snake said.

Snake quickly stopped me in my tracks, like my identity was some sort of secret. I guess if I said too much, it might have been incriminating for him as well.

"You're right, she doesn't need to explain. You do. So, what were you doing there with this stripper?" Danielle asked, stepping a little closer to Snake and me with her arms folded.

I stood and balled-up my fist, ready to attack. I had to show this female that she might've needed to take a second thought on making the wrong move. She stepped back and stood a little closer to Snake, as if he would provide some sort of protective shield to keep her from getting her ass kicked. I realized this little scary chick wasn't any threat at all. Her bark was surely more vicious than her bite.

"I'll take it from here, thanks." Danielle rolled her eyes then squeezed between Snake and me.

The little bitch only wanted some attention, and it almost cost her an ass-beating. Once I saw that she posed no real threat, I didn't resist. I got up silently and walked to another bench at the corner. I watched as they entered the hospital and disappeared behind the emergency room door. There were many people around the bench smoking cigarettes. As stressed as I was, I figured I would try one myself.

"Excuse me. May I have a cigarette, please?" I asked an attractive young girl who was obviously just as stressed as I.

"Help yourself," she said as she handed me the entire pack, never even looking up.

Every so often she would open her cell phone, begin to dial a number then hang up. I wondered what worries such a young girl could have. The curiosity was killing me.

"Looks like you're having a hard time making that phone call," I stated, hoping she would tell me what was bothering her so.

The young girl finally looked up. She too examined me from head to toe.

"Looks like you're having an even worse time than me. You're covered in blood. What happened?" she asked, catching me totally off guard.

I didn't expect her to come so direct. I actually found myself smiling at her aggressiveness.

"You're right, sweetie. I've had a hell of a day. Now, why don't you tell me about your day? Why are you so sad?" I asked.

"Look, lady, maybe you should just mind your business," she said as she burst into tears.

I rubbed her shoulder. She obviously wasn't as tough as she portrayed. Another one whose bark was much more vicious than her bite. I was beginning to wonder if it was contagious and I was a carrier.

"It's okay, honey. I know exactly how you feel. Just let it all out."

She finally told her story.

"There were only three people in my life who loved me as much as I love them. I've already lost one, and I may lose the other two today. And even worse, it may be my fault," she continued to explain. "My boyfriend, Duke, and my cousin, Ray-Ray, had a shoot-out at the Coliseum today, and maybe I could have prevented it. But I didn't ease the bad blood between them, and this is what it led to. I've even lost my best friend because of this. She dates my cousin, and I don't even have the courage to call her and tell her the bad news."

I felt a special connection with this young lady as we talked. She reminded me a lot of myself. I consoled her, ultimately giving her the courage she needed to call her friend. I assured her she wasn't alone in anything she was going through. And for every situation she was experiencing, there was someone worse off than she was. One thing I could promise her was that troubles don't last forever.

As we spoke, I didn't bother telling her I knew Duke or that I was present at the shooting. She would want details of the event, and I didn't think that was in her best interest at the moment. I finished my cigarette and called one of my girls from the club to take me to my car.

"Yeah, bitch!" My girl Storm answered the phone in her usual snappy tone.

"Hey. I need you to come pick my up from the hospital."

"Girl, why? What happened? Oh shit—you was at the Coliseum! Don't tell me you were in the middle of that shit. Girl, you a'ight?" Storm spat question after question.

I was not in the mood for explaining at the moment, so I had to think fast.

"We'll talk as soon as you get here," I promised. I knew that would guarantee my ride to the Coliseum. The shit a nosy bitch would do for news. The day had been too draining for me. I longed for a hot shower and good night's sleep.

Once I ended my conversation with Storm, I picked up where I left off with the young lady.

"I feel like I have a certain connection with you. You remind me so much of myself. I know you don't know me from Eve, so let me introduce myself. I'm Ceazia." I extended my hand.

"I'm BJ. Nice to meet you, Ceazia." She shook my hand.

"If you ever need anyone to talk to, please feel free to call me." I patted her on the back and gave her my number before leaving.

CHUNICHI

I headed back toward the emergency room. I wanted to say a few words to Snake before leaving, and check on Duke's well-being.

I entered the waiting area. Snake, along with several other family members and friends, was in the conference room speaking with the doctor.

"Duke has several gunshot wounds to his upper body. We're prepping him for the operating room now. We expect the surgery to last approximately eight hours. There is a waiting room on the sixth floor. The immediate family can wait there for counsel with the surgeon after the surgery is over."

The questions began to overflow as soon as the doctor ended his sentence. Snake was still silent, just as before. I wanted so badly to comfort him, but his lady friend stood close by. Rather than disturb the peace, I left the emergency room unnoticed and waited outside for my girlfriend.

CHAPTER 14

BAD NEWS

CHUNICHI

GINA

Ring, ring . . . ring, ring . . . ring, ring . . .

I was awakened by the constant ringing of the phone. I was shocked at the name I saw on the caller ID. It read: JASMINE SMITH

"Hel-lo!" I yelled into the phone.

I didn't understand why this bitch would be calling me. I hadn't called BJ since our falling out. That should've been her clue I didn't have no love for her. She had the nerve to come back defensively.

"I'm not calling you about any beef, Gina—" BJ began to say before I cut her off.

"I know you're not. You ain't that damn brave. You got me once, but believe me, bitch, it ain't over. The next time I see you, that's your ass!"

After my spill, I gave BJ a chance to speak. I was fired up, and I was ready for any response she could come back with.

"Well, maybe you can beat my ass at Norfolk General Hospital. I thought you might want to know Ray-Ray's been shot. He's here at the hospital, and he's in critical condition."

That was not a response I'd expected, nor was I prepared for it. A silence fell over the phone as my brain began to race.

This can't be true. I just spoke to him. He's fine. This is a game. She's trying to get back at me. But what if she's telling the truth? Who would do such a thing? Maybe she had Duke set him up. But I know she wouldn't do that to her own cousin. What the hell is going on?

109

My thinking was interrupted by BJ's cry.

"He's . . . he's . . . not going to make it, Gina. He's not going to make it."

I could feel the pain in BJ's voice. My heart sank as she continued to tell me the story of Ray-Ray's shooting. I wanted so badly to know that this was all just a ploy to hurt me, but I knew this wasn't a game. She was telling the truth. I began to remember my dream and the shots I'd heard. I hung up the phone immediately. I ran around the house frantically as I grabbed clothes and my purse. I knew exactly where I last placed my mom's keys, so I grabbed them and headed to her car.

"God, please let this car start. God, please let this car start," I prayed as I jumped in. A few pumps on the gas, a few bangs on the steering wheel, and a few profanities later, I was on my way to the hospital.

I ran through the emergency room doors and spotted BJ along with her aunt and other family members. My heart was already in the pit of my stomach from the moment I listened to BJ on the phone. After noticing the saddened faces of Ray-Ray's family, reality set in.

"Noooooo!" I screamed as BJ's words repeated in my head. *He's not going to make it . . . he's not going to make it . . . he's not going to make it.*

BJ rushed over and grabbed me as the strength left my body, and I collapsed to the floor.

"Please tell me he's fine, BJ. Tell me he's fine." I begged her to promise he was still living.

I looked at her for a response but she didn't answer. I grabbed her shirt and began to shake her.

"Do you hear me? I know you hear me, you bitch! Tell me he's fine. Tell me he's fine!" I yelled at the top of my lungs.

Again she didn't respond. She just stood motionless as tears rolled down her face. I ignored her pain and lashed out at her verbally.

"This is all your fault, you bitch! You started this beef!" I blabbed, full of anger.

"How could you say that, Gina? Their beef was behind you and your cheating ways. You're to blame, bitch! I'm losing a cousin and a boyfriend! What the fuck are you losing?" BJ shot back at me.

"I'm losing a baby father. You're the reason my child is not going to have a father, BJ!" I yelled in rage.

"You're pregnant?" BJ said in a soft whisper.

"Yes, I am, and thanks to you I will be a single mom," I yelled back.

Deep inside, I knew BJ was not at fault, but I had no one else to blame. My life was destroyed. Ray-Ray was the only person left in my life that I trusted.

The people in the emergency room lobby listened as BJ and I argued back and forth. They could only wonder why we had so much anger and why we blamed each other. I looked to my right and noticed Duke's brother and other family members standing silently as spectators. Looking for anyone to blame, I quickly made them my next target.

"And that's the family of the murderer! Maybe you should stand over there, BJ!" I shouted while pointing at Duke's family.

Immediately, people from both families stood up. My crying was interrupted by fear, because the tension quickly thickened in the room. Given the hostile situation, I knew exactly what was next.

No one said a word, but all of a sudden they erupted, and there was a huge fight. Chairs were flying, people were screaming, and many of us were crying beyond control. The hospital security was almost worthless, but good thing the police detectives were handy in calling for back-up. In the meantime, the detectives were in the middle of the chaos, breaking things up in no time. They managed to separate the families with threats of handcuffs and jail time. Once again, police arrived on the scene, we were given ultimatums against what most of us wanted. We were forced to go home if we weren't members of the victims' immediate family.

Once home, I thought about the last time Ray-Ray and I spoke. It was breaking my heart as I reflected back to my phone call to Ray-Ray earlier in the day.

When I was awakened from my sleep by the sound of gunshots, it must have been intuition. Ray-Ray was getting shot just at that moment. Then when I called him and heard the words "I love you," those were his final words to me. Instead of me trusting my man or assuming something must be wrong, I assumed he was cheating. I was angry for no real reason. The last word he may have heard from me was hate. And now he's gone. Ray-Ray I'm sorry. I love you, baby. I'm carrying our baby, and I know you will always be here through our child.

I cried from the paralyzing pain of the day's events. The thought of living another day without Ray-Ray was unbearable. I never knew such a terrible day would come. Nothing could've ever prepared me for this trauma. Sadly, I had no one I could lean on. I wanted so badly to go into my mother's room and crawl into the bed with her, but I knew better than to expect her to understand my hurt. After coming home to tell her about my pregnancy, Ray-Ray's death, and the drama at the hospital, all my mother was concerned about was her car and the fact I'd taken it without her permission. She also threw out her thoughts on my choices in men.

"You mess with all the wrong guys anyway, Gina. That boy didn't mean you no good. Whatcha want me to say? And now you done got yourself pregnant, and he ain't gon' be around to help you. You shoulda seen it comin', Gina, 'cause that boy wasn't nothing but a no-good hustler. Everybody knows that gaming ways only gets a hustler time in jail or the grave. You made your bed hard, now you gon' have to lay in it. Give me my damn keys, and it better not be a scratch on my car."

I felt defeated, and was ready to give up on life and love. My first mind was to disrespect my momma by cussing her out and throwing up her bad choices in men, too. Bubba was far from being a saint, and deep down, momma knew he was guilty for raping me. Momma's words hurt, and I wished she would've spared me them at the moment.

MARRIED TO THE GAME

Every time I tried to forget about how much betrayal I'd experienced in my young life, something else would happen to keep me on the path of mistrust. I wanted to hate my mother for not being there for me in all my times of need, but my heart wouldn't let me.

I stayed in my room the rest of the day, unable to sleep. I was weak from crying and not eating. I cried so much my brain began to pound. Although my stomach was empty, I swallowed four extra-strength Tylenols in a desperate attempt for relief. Besides, I was certain taking such a large quantity of pills at one time would place me into the sleeping mode for which I longed. It seemed I made the right decision, because within a matter of minutes, I was off to sleep.

CHAPTER 15

THE CROSSROADS

UNKNOWN MAN

It's always sad when you lose a young soldier, but that's life on the streets. Death has no age. I felt sorrier for those two little girls more than anything. It was sad BJ had to lose a cousin and a best friend. And then that chick Gina lost her child's father. It was fucked up they had to be out there like that, but when you get involved in the game, it's an eye for an eye situation. No one cares about the losses. They just tryin' to get you before you get them.

Ray-Ray's funeral was huge. They really laced the li'l nigga. He had Benz stretch limos, a gold-trimmed casket, and was buried in one of the nicest cemeteries in Virginia Beach. His line of cars leaving the church to the gravesite was at least three miles long. He was really doing it for a young buck. His shit was better than some of the OGs from the hood.

I guess you never know how many people really love you until you gone or on your death bed. I had no idea that li'l nigga had so much love on the streets. Of course, there were at least five chicks there claiming to be his girl. Luckily, Gina was the only one carrying his baby. And his family knew she was the main chick, so she was treated as such. She rode in the limo, sat on the front pew, and all that first lady shit. I was amazed to see her and BJ consoling each other during the funeral. I would think after the hospital drama that they would be at each other's throats even more than before. It's crazy how a death can change things in

116

an instant.

I had no idea so many niggas that was supposed to be on Snake's team was friends with Ray-Ray too. I saw a lot of cats at his funeral that wasn't supposed to be there. I saw there were a few niggas I would have to keep my eye on. They seemed to be playing both sides of the fence. Things on the streets were about to be ugly.

CHAPTER 16

WATER UNDER THE BRIDGE

BJ

It had been two years since Ray-Ray's death, and things between Gina and I had not progressed very much. I mean, there was no beef, but we just didn't have that bond like we used to. The only time I saw her was when she brought the baby over on the weekend and on birthdays and holidays. She looked terrible, and she always seemed depressed. From what I heard, since Ray's death, she hadn't even dated anyone. It broke my heart to see her in that condition, and that's why I was making it my personal duty to repair our friendship.

When the doorbell of grandmother's house rang, I knew it could only be Gina. She brought the baby over each Friday like clockwork. I was excited to see my little kinfolk.

"Hey, RJ," I said, giving Ray, Jr., a kiss on the cheek.

"He's been a little cranky today, so he may be sick. I packed some meds for him, two sets of outfits for each day and—"

"Gina, I know the spill. You've been bringing him over here, saying the same thing for quite some time now," I said, cutting her off.

Gina looked at me in amazement, but she didn't say a word. I wondered what could be going through her mind, but I was used to her not having much to say. I didn't think it was intentional, though. Gina was just so different than she was before Ray-Ray's death, but I wanted the old Gina back. I tried to hold a conversation with her in an effort to get her to open up like she did back in the day.

"So, what have you got planned for this weekend?" I asked as I took RJ from her arms.

"Nothing. Just going to clean the house and get caught up on some things," she stated, avoiding eye contact with me.

I knew she was lonely, and since it was now my personal duty to get the old Gina back, I invited her to a night out.

"Well, I've been invited to a little gathering tonight, and you could come if you like."

"No. I don't have any money or anything to wear," she stated, quickly denying my offer.

I was ready for her rejection, so I came back with a rebuttal. "No problem. I'll pay your way, and you can borrow something of mine to wear," I suggested.

The past couple of years had been lovely for me since Duke had stepped his game up. I had plenty of things she could wear. I even had shit that still had the tags on them. I'd shop for nothing but the best. I owned gear ranging from Gucci to Versace to Luis Vuitton to Chanel. All of my handbags were name brand too.

Gina had seen how clean I could dress, so I knew she figured I had something she'd like to put on. As a matter of fact, I was sure she'd like this new Donna Karan outfit I'd never worn. I described the set to Gina, and then I finally witnessed her face lighting up. However, it was tough convincing Gina to enjoy herself for a change.

"Oh, I don't know, BJ." Gina sighed.

"I just would really like to spend some time with you, Gina. I miss you," I said sincerely as I gave her a small hug.

Amazingly, the hug was all it took to finally put a smile on Gina's face. When I let her go, her face was more relaxed and she had a pleasant gleam that accompanied her smile. She agreed to hang out with me, so we set plans to meet at her home around eleven. I offered to drive since Duke recently bought me a brand new Acura TL. Gina nodded as she seemed pleased with my offer.

I ran in the house to call Ceazia. I'd been in touch with her since the day I met her at the hospital. Since BJ and I were no longer best friends, Ceazia had become the big sister and best friend I never had. We talked every day, sometimes two or three times a day. I told her everything I was going through, and she told me everything there was to know about living the life as a gangster's girl.

"Hey, Li'l Momma," she said just after picking up.

Li'l Momma was a nickname Ceazia had given me. Ceazia said she liked kickin' it with me because I was really mature for my age, and that she thought of me as a little woman. She started out teasing me by calling me Li'l Momma, but it soon turned into a welcomed compliment.

"Hey, C. Just called to tell you I'll be at the party tonight, and I'm bringing Gina with me," I excitedly told her.

"Oh, so you were able to convince her to come, huh? How'd that happen?" she asked.

"I guess it was timing. I was just as shocked as you are now, but needless to say, I'm happy we're going to be mending our friendship."

"You know what, Li'l Momma . . . I'm glad to hear this about you and Gina. This is what you've been wanting, and it's good to know Gina is finally coming around."

I'd often told Ceazia how much I missed Gina and wanted our friendship back, so she encouraged me to go out and get it. She was thrilled to know I'd actually achieved the first step. We finished up our conversation and agreed to see each other later.

Next, I called Duke. I was eager to tell him the good news too.

The phone rang continuously. Like every day, I could never reach Duke on the first try. So I tried calling again. And again. And again. That was my final attempt. I dialed up his business phone.

"BJ! This betta be a fucking emergency! You know I don't want you hitting me up on this line!" he yelled into the phone.

"No, it's not an emergency, but this is the only way I can contact your ass. I've told you over and over again if you don't answer your phone when I call, it scares me. I have no choice but to think you're dead or in jail," I said, leaving out my real thought of him cheating.

"Yeah, and I told you if I don't answer then I'm obviously busy!"

"Well, with the line of business you're in, I just can't assume you're okay. Just learn to answer the phone, please?" I begged.

"Yeah, okay. What is it, baby? I'm in the middle of some business right now," he said calmly.

I liked when my man softened up to me just after me begging him for something. I got goosebumps when he called me baby. He knew I liked when he call me sweet pet names.

"Well, I just wanted you to know that I'm going out tonight with Ceazia and Gina," I said with pride.

"What? What the fuck I tell you about that bitch, Ceazia? And when the hell did you start fucking with Gina again? I know you didn't call me thinking I'd be happy about hearing this shit," Duke said angrily.

The sweetness had just flown out the window when I admitted my plans to Duke. There was something about Ceazia that Duke just didn't like. I didn't know what it was about her, but Duke despised me being around her. He even hated the sound of her name. I asked over and over again why he disliked Ceazia so much, and all he could tell me was that she was trouble or that she couldn't be trusted or that she was shiesty. But he never gave me anything concrete to help explain why he said those things.

Duke had pissed me off with his attitude, so I gave him one right back. "Duke, I'm going out with both of my friends tonight! And I've started back fucking with Gina as of today," I said before hanging up.

I didn't want to give Duke anymore room for rebuttal. My mind was made up, and I didn't want him to blow my excitement with more negative thoughts. I knew me hanging up the phone on him was grounds for more argument. But at least I knew that would have to wait because I remembered Duke mentioning he was taking care of some business when I called.

With a wonderful night ahead of me, I opened my closet doors and sat on the bed. I'd arranged my closet so perfectly that all I had to do was sit on the bed and open both sides of the closet and I could see everything. I had my shoes in plastic boxes with pictures on each, my belts hanging from tie racks, and clothes sorted by item. All the jeans were together, short sleeve shirts, cargo pants, long sleeve shirts, dresses—it was perfect. It took me no time to find the perfect outfit for myself. Now it was time for Gina.

Since Gina had the baby, we were around the same size. Always wanting to show emphasis on the good stuff and hide the bad, I chose stretch jeans for Gina rather than the Donna Karan outfit I originally had in mind. She finally had an ass, and I wanted her to flaunt it, but she also had a small pudge in the front that we needed to hide. Stretch jeans were perfect for that because it gripped the ass just right but squeezed the tummy. Then I found her a perfect baby-doll top to show off her breasts and again hide the pudge. The top was a tube, cupping her breasts, but the bottom flowed like a shirt dress. The outfit was perfect. Now she just needed the perfect accessories. I prayed she had some nice sandals and a bag. I could help her with a purse, but sandals were out of the question. Gina had feet the size of Andre the Giant. I crossed my fingers and called her up.

"Hello?" she answered on the first ring.

"Hey, girl. I found the perfect outfit for you, but I just need to know if you have some white sandals and a bag to match."

"Yeah, I think so. I haven't been anywhere in so long, I'm not sure what I have anymore," she said pathetically.

"Okay, cool. Well, take a look and if not, just let me know what you do have. Maybe we can work with that."

"All right, girl. I'm going to take a quick nap. Just call me before you come," she stated before hanging up.

CHAPTER 17

FOREVER HAUNTED

GINA

I looked in my closet to find shoes and a bag. It had been so long since I'd gone anyplace nice, that I wasn't sure what I owned anymore. I reluctantly searched through the clothes and shoes that were thrown all over the floor. At least a year had passed since I last went through that stuff. I'd made it a custom of wearing sweatpants, T-shirts and sneakers on a regular basis.

I searched as though I was looking for a pot of gold, throwing old shoes and clothes in every direction. I came across things that I hadn't seen in years. I smiled as I picked up one of RJ's newborn tees. Staring at that T made me remember how small and precious RJ was as a newborn. He was, and always had been, everything I could imagine my child to be. I hugged the picture of my son, admiring how much RJ resembled his dad at birth, and even more so now.

I soon came across a picture of me and BJ. I was surprised to see how much she and I had changed in our appearances.

"Wow, was I small back then!" I stated as I took a moment to exam my small frame.

I continued to search, finding everything except a nice pair of sandals and a bag. I was deep inside my closet near the final corner; there was no hope. Just as I was about to give up, I came across a Bloomingdale's shopping bag. I wondered where it could have come from as I pulled it out. I was sure I never purchased anything there. Hell, Norfolk didn't even have a Bloomingdale's, and I hadn't been outside the Seven Cities my entire life.

Maybe it's something that belongs to my mom, I thought as I opened the bag. There were two large wrapped gifts, a smaller gift, and a card. I opened the bag with caution, starting with the card. It was a birthday card signed from Ray-Ray. Tears began to well in my eyes as I opened the gifts. It was sandals with a matching bag, and a necklace with a diamond locket. I opened the locket to find a picture of Ray-Ray and me inside.

I sat on the floor, thinking. It was my birthday gift from Ray-Ray, and it had been sitting in my closet since his death. He must have hid it from me, but he never got to tell me because he was killed. This was a pleasant surprise, but I still couldn't believe it. It's crazy how things come together.

I called BJ to tell her the news. She was just as stunned as I was about the revelation.

"Gina, you've got to be kidding me. Really? After all this time, you're just now finding your birthday surprise?" BJ pondered.

"Yes, and I know it sounds strange, but I just had no idea Ray-Ray had hidden these things so far back in the closet. Had you not asked me to go out, I still wouldn't have found the bag."

"So, talk. How do you feel? Are you happy?"

"Yes. But I also feel guilty, BJ."

"Why, Gina? You are my girl, and I wish for things to be the way they used to be between us. You can still talk to me."

I sighed before answering BJ. "Ray-Ray pissed me off after I gave him the news of my pregnancy.

After thinking long and hard about how upset he made me, I tried to call him to set things straight. Once I reached him, I could hear faint sounds of what sounded like Ray-Ray and another woman having sex. I later realized he wasn't betraying me after all. What I heard was his dying words to me." I began to cry. BJ tried to calm me down.

"Gina, everything is going to be okay. Talk it out. What did Ray-Ray say to you?"

I continued to sob in between breaths. "He . . . said . . . he . . . told . . . me . . . he . . . loved . . . me." I could barely speak as my voice trembled through my sadness.

"Gina, everything is going to be okay. I understand that accepting Ray-Ray's death is a bit hard, but I also know that he still lives."

I was confused. "Huh? What are you talking about, BJ?"

"Don't you feel him? Don't you see him, Gina? When you hold the beautiful son you birthed into this world, don't you feel close to Ray-Ray?"

"Yes. I know what you mean, because I do see Ray-Ray when I look into my baby's eyes."

"I know you do, because I can see him too. Please try to be strong, Gina. RJ needs you."

BJ and I spent more moments on the phone lifting each other up. After our conversation, I couldn't help but reflect back to the day Ray-Ray was killed. I remembered the dreadful phone call I received from BJ.

I thought you may want to know Ray-Ray has been shot. He's here at the hospital and he's in critical condition. He's . . . he's . . . not going to make it, Gina. He's not going to make it.

BJ just couldn't understand how much those words haunted me every day. There were so many things that reminded me of Ray-Ray. I looked at the picture of us in the locket then thought of our son, RJ. He looked just like his father, and I knew Ray would have been a wonderful father. We would have been a perfect little family. I would have given my son everything I never had. Me and Ray would have given RJ all the love and care I never had.

All the events in the past hour had become overwhelming, so I took a generous amount of my prescription medications in an attempt to take a little nap before our night out. It had become routine for me to take sleeping pills and Prozac on a daily basis, sometimes two or three times. After Ray-Ray's death, I couldn't function properly. I wasn't eating like I should, and a good night's sleep was almost impossible due to nightmares. I couldn't even communicate well anymore. I mainly stared at people, unable to bring myself to talk without crying, so my mom admitted me to the local crisis unit. After months of counseling and for the sake of my child, I was finally able to live a regular life with the help of plenty of daily medications. Little did people know that my sleeping pill, in great doses, was how I managed to cope with things.

Dear God, please take this pain away from me. Dear God, please take this pain away from me. I repeated as I tried to fall asleep. This too had become a nightly routine.

Nothing could fill the void in my heart, and

when I'd drift off to sleep is when my heart would ache the most. The nightmares kept the memory of Ray-Ray's death fresh. The continuous pain of losing him was like no other pain I ever felt before. It hurt, it ached, and it was a pain so deep any amount of medication or level of sedation I tried couldn't ease it. So, I steadily increased the amounts of meds, hoping I'd soon find the needed dosage.

Tears rolled down my cheeks each time I thought of Ray-Ray. I called his phone every day, sometimes twice a day, knowing there would be no answer, but with hopes there would be. I never disconnected his phone, just so I could hear his sweet voice. Yet each time the voicemail answered, it was a constant reminder he was gone. He was no longer here with me; he was no longer sleeping in my bed next to me. I rolled over and there was no warm body beside me, yet there was a fresh scent of D & G cologne on my pillowcase. I kept a bottle of the cologne and sprayed it on the pillow each night, just as another desperate attempt to fall asleep. But again, that too just became another reminder he was gone. I hugged the pillow tight as I fell asleep. It was a feeble replacement for the man that would usually lay there.

Ring, ring!

I jumped at the sound of the telephone with hopes of seeing the words WIRELESS CALLER across the screen of the caller ID. Instead, it read something other. I ignored the remaining rings as the realization sank.

It isn't him, and it never will be him.

MARRIED TO THE GAME

These tears would always burn my face at night, the scent of his cologne would always haunt me, my heart would remain empty, and I would continue to pray each night, *Dear God, please take this pain away from me. Dear God, please take this pain away from me. DEAR GOD, PLEASE TAKE THIS PAIN AWAY FROM ME.*

CHAPTER 18

GIRLS GONE WILD

BJ

I called Gina's house for the twentieth time. Each time I called, her voicemail came on. I knew things were too good to be true. All she had to do was tell me she no longer wanted to go out. I didn't even bother leaving her a message. I just got dressed and headed straight to the club. I was determined to have a good night, with or without Gina. As soon as I pulled up to the club, I noticed C standing out front.

"Hey, girlie!" I yelled as I parked the car and headed toward her.

"Hey, Li'l Momma," she stated, giving me a tight hug and a long kiss on the cheek as though she hadn't seen me in years. C always seemed to be so touchy-feely. She had to be the most affectionate female I knew.

C continued to introduce me to all of her friends, who all were very pretty and dressed very nice, I must add. I felt privileged to even be welcomed around such a high-class clique.

Once in the club, eyes immediately were on us. Guys began to flock from every direction. I'd never seen anything like this before. I felt like a celebrity. Not once did we even go to the bar. Guys were sending drinks to our table left and right. We had everything from continuous glasses of Hypnotiq and Absolut to bottles of Moet sent to our table. I was loving it! It wasn't long before the combination of alcohol and reggae had me going. After one last drink, none of us could sit still any longer.

134

Everyone headed to the dance floor, full of energy. Once on the floor we all moved to the tunes of the reggae rhythms, once again drawing the attention of everyone in the club. I observed the sexy moves C did as she danced seductively. I was intrigued with how precisely she moved her hips. It seemed so natural. I studied every move, making a mental note. As she danced, I noticed one of her girlfriends come behind her and dance along. Then I looked at the other girls to see if they noticed, but to my surprise, they were doing the same. Unsure how to react, I left the dance floor in a hurry. I immediately went to the bar to order a bottle of water. I figured maybe I was a little too drunk and needed to sober up a bit. Maybe things weren't how they seemed. I could have been overreacting. I sipped my water slowly as I stood at the bar alone.

"Wha gwan?" a sexy baritone voice said to me in patois.

"Hi," I said, timidly examining the fine, dark Jamaican man that stood before me. His skin was as dark as rich chocolate and his smile was as white as snow. His broad six-foot frame towered over me as he spoke.

"So yuh down like di gal dem yuh roll wit?" he asked, confirming things were just as they seemed.

So it wasn't the alcohol, after all. I wasn't tripping. That explained C's affectionate side.

"No, I don't get down like that," I replied very sternly, in an attempt to let him know ain't shit jumping off.

"Yeh, mi would like fi give yuh mi number," he offered.

"Hey, Judah," Storm, one of Ceazia's friend's, said seductively while pinching him on his side and interrupting our conversation.

"Whappen, Storm? Whappen, Cinnamon?" he responded with little emotion then directed his attention back to me.

I noticed he greeted C by her stage name, which could only mean one thing. He knew her from the strip club.

"Wha yuh name?" the sexy Jamaican asked.

"Her name is BJ, and she is too young for you," Storm snapped while putting her arm around my neck as though she was protecting me from some sort of beast.

"Wha mek yuh so sure?"

"'Cause she's Cinnamon's *little* sister. Besides, you need someone in the major leagues for the games you like to play," Storm responded while giving him a seductive look.

By this time, the whole entourage was off the dance floor and surrounding us. They all seemed to know Judah, as they called him, very well. Although he didn't seem too interested in any of them, they all flocked around him and he purchased each one of them a drink. Tired of all the commotion from the night, I decided it was time to go home. I said my good-byes to everyone and headed out.

Once in my car, I pulled out my cell phone and called Duke. Like every other time I called, he didn't answer.

There was a knock at my window, nearly scaring the hell out of me. I looked up and saw

Judah.

"What's up?" I asked as I cracked my window just enough to talk.

"Whappen, yuh nuh have mi number."

Since I already had my phone out, I took his number and promised to call. Before leaving, he told me I could find him at this club every Thursday through Saturday, to give him a call and he'd let me in free. I was flattered by his kindness.

When he left, I pulled off and tried calling Duke's phone over and over again. Then entire ride to my house I called him, but there was no answer. This time, I didn't even bother calling his business phone. Once I got in the house, I took a bath and tried calling Gina to tell her how much fun she missed out on. Again, I only got her voicemail. I began to think it was me. Maybe she really wasn't feeling me after all. Well, I knew she would have to come for RJ, and I'd just wait to speak to her then.

Since I was still awake, I made another hopeless attempt to contact Duke. I tried to force myself to sleep as I thought about the events of the night. I reminisced about how it felt to be on top of the world and to have all eyes on me in the club. I played C's dance moves over and over in my head as I mimicked them while I lay on the bed. Then I thought about Jamaican Judah and how sexy he was as he spoke to me in his baritone voice. His attire wasn't the average Rasta attire I'd often seen on many reggae music videos. Instead, he dressed very neatly and wore the latest labels. I figured he was involved with the club somehow. He seemed to be pretty popular among the club-goers and quite generous with the patrons as well. Normally, I wouldn't have taken his number, but how could I refuse such a sexy, well-mannered man?

After several minutes of thinking, I still was not able to force myself to sleep, so I tried calling Duke one last time. But this time his phone was off; straight to voicemail every time. That was the last straw. I only had one option left—go by his house. I hopped up and threw on a sweatsuit and headed out the door. I was at his house within ten minutes. I circled the neighborhood twice for surveillance before pulling into his court. I couldn't believe my eyes as I pulled up.

"Please don't let this be as it seems," I said as I parked my car a couple of houses down and walked toward Duke's home.

The closer I got to his house, the clearer things became. Just what I hoped wasn't true had come to light. A white 745LI, chrome factories, and paper tags; only one like it in the area.

"C, you shiesty bitch!" I said as I walked toward her car, getting angrier with every step.

Now it all made sense. That's why Duke pretended to hate her so much. That's why he didn't want me around her. That's why C's first advice to me was to leave Duke when I would talk to her about our problems. All the times she told me I was too good for him and now look! They were afraid shit would hit the fan. Despite all their efforts to keep shit in the closet, it still came out and shit was going to hit the fan in ways they never expected.

I pulled out my shank and stabbed each one of

C's tires as I walked around her car, contemplating my next move. My first thought was to go on a rampage and bust her windows, kick dents in her car, spray paint all over it, then go in the house and whip her conniving, stripping ass. But then I thought things through. If I was to do those things, it would probably be Duke to fix them, and then they would be right back were they left off. No damage done, for real. That wasn't good enough. I needed a plan, a plan of revenge that would really make a difference. I needed time to devise the perfect revenge, so I decided to leave, but not before I walked to Duke's car and slit his tires too. Hey, I had to let off a little steam!

"This will do for now. I have something more in store for these two," I said with a frown across my face as I returned to my car unnoticed.

I thought long and hard as I went back to my house. I was so hurt I couldn't cry. I had too much anger. I wasn't sure what I was going to do, but one thing I was sure of was that I planned to move slowly. Like a snake in the grass, I would sneak up on them and attack when they least expected it. This would be the sweetest revenge ever.

When I got home, I couldn't sleep. The thought of Duke and my so-called big sister fucking haunted my mind. I began to think maybe this was what I deserved for the fucked up shit I'd done to Gina years ago. I fucked Duke when he was with her, and now C was returning the favor and fucking him while he was with me. Now I knew how it felt.

To this day, Gina had no idea I'd fucked Duke

behind her back. I felt it was time to come clean. I tried calling her house again, this time from my grandmother's line. I knew if she saw that number, she would definitely answer in fear that something may be wrong with RJ. But to my surprise, she didn't answer. Now, that certainly was not like Gina. Something had to be wrong. I tried calling again and again to be sure she wasn't just sleeping, but still I got no response. So once again, I put on my sweatsuit and headed out, this time to Gina's house.

I knew she was home because her car was out front. I banged on the door repeatedly, but there was no answer. I headed to retrieve the spare key she always kept under the welcome mat at the back door. I grabbed the key and quickly unlocked the door. I knew she would be mad, but this was a risk I was willing to take. Something was telling me Gina was not okay.

"Gina!" I yelled from the back door.

When there was no response, I immediately headed to her bedroom while continuously calling her name.

I walked in the room to see Gina sound asleep. She was okay. I sighed in relief. I didn't understand how someone could sleep so hard, but I was relieved just to see that she was okay. As I walked toward her bed, I noticed a bottle of prescription medication on the nightstand. I figured she'd taken her meds and that's why she was sleeping so soundly. I grabbed her blanket and pulled it over her. As I pulled the blanket up, I noticed her body felt stiff and cold.

CHUNICHI

"Gina!" I yelled in a panic while shaking her.

There was still no response. She didn't move. She wasn't waking up. I grabbed the phone and dialed 911.

"Please, God, help her. Please, God, don't let her leave me. God, please!" I repeated over and over as I cried on the phone with the emergency operator.

The EMTs arrived in no time. They quickly came in the room, forcing me out as they attempted to revive Gina. Minutes seemed like hours as I sat in the living room of her home, pacing back and forth.

"Miss Smith?" the paramedic called as he walked from the bedroom, taking off his gloves.

"Yes," I answered, nervous about the news I may hear.

"I'm sorry. She didn't make it."

My body froze in disbelief. This was too much for me to handle. The words the paramedics were speaking to me began to slur, the room began to spin; there were spots before my eyes.

Flop!

I was out like a light, passed out on the floor.

The past few weeks had been a living hell. I hadn't gone out of the house once, not even for Gina's funeral. I hadn't seen sunlight or smelled the rain. I felt like my life was over. I didn't know what I'd done to deserve such a bad hand in life.

I hadn't even talked with Duke or C, although the pain of their deceit had really set in by now. They still had no idea I knew their secret, and I

141

had no plans of revealing it. They just figured my isolation was due to Gina's death.

As I got up to bathe I examined myself in the mirror. My hair was knotty and stood on top of my head. That beautiful, young, natural glow was gone, replaced with an elderly ash. I couldn't stand the sight before me. I had to do something. In an attempt to make myself feel better, I filled the tub with hot water and aromatherapy bath beads, turned off the lights, lit candles all around the bathtub and soaked, while listening to the relaxing tunes of Usher.

Thirty minutes later, I felt revived. I grabbed my phone and began to dial Duke's number, but hung up before I hit the final digit. I still wasn't prepared to speak to him. Yet, I desired the companionship of someone. My lover was gone, my big sister was gone, and now the only friend I ever had was gone. There was no one to turn to. As I sat on the bed, nearly back to the point of depression that I started from, I thought about Judah. What more perfect time than now to call him? I dialed his number slowly, hoping he would still remember me.

"Hello?" Judah said in the baritone voice just as sexy as the first night I met him.

"Hi, Judah. It's BJ. I met you at The Mango Tree a few weeks ago," I said, praying he would remember me.

I really didn't have the energy to play the "let me refresh your memory" game. Hell, if he didn't remember me, then that would be an indication that he gave his number out a little too often for my taste.

"Wha gwan, BJ? I'm glad to hear from you," he responded, sounding excited that I called.

"I'm sorry it took so long for me to call, but I had to do a thorough background check on you before I called. I had to make sure you weren't some sort of psycho or rapist or terrorist or something." I lied, not wanting to let him in on all the drama I had in my life the past few weeks. That would definitely be a turn-off.

"Mi tek it mi clear? Background check came back okay?"

"Sure did. So now it's safe for us to spend some time. Are you going to be at The Mango Tree tonight?" I asked, hoping that I could come out and have a few drinks on him to ease my mind.

Since Duke and I hadn't been talking, my money was looking kind of funny, which was just another motivator. I really needed to make some moves just on the strength of financial stability, if nothing else.

"Every Thursday through Sunday. You coming out tonight?"

"Sure, why not? I have nothing else to do. So, what exactly do you do there?"

"I play music and throw different parties. We refer to it as a sound. The name of my sound is Macten Sound. We're based here, New York, Florida, Atlanta, and Jamaica."

"Sounds interesting. I guess that's why you're so popular," I stated, trying to inquire about his dealings with C and her girls without being too obvious.

"Popular with whom? Your girls from the other night?" he said, picking up on exactly what I was trying to say.

"No, not just them. I mean in general. But since you mentioned them, how do you know them, anyway? They seemed really interested in you," I stated just to see if he would lie.

"I know them from the strip club. They aren't really interested in me. It's just that I'm pretty generous with them at the club. And I hire a couple of them on a regular basis. You know how it is. It's their job to get money, so they're always on the grind. But that's as far as it goes. No relationships or anything—strictly business. So, just how close are you and Cinnamon?"

Not wanting to let him in on the grime of that little bitch, I pretended that things were still good between us.

"Oh, C? She's my girl! The way we met was wild, but we've been friends for the past couple of years. She's like a big sister to me," I lied.

Just the mention of her name was pissing me off, and it took all I had to force those words out. In an attempt to end the conversation before the animosity began to show, I told Judah I had to run some errands and I would see him later in the night. I hung up the phone, feeling revived and eager to see him.

CHAPTER 19

HEAR NO EVIL, SPEAK NO EVIL

MARRIED TO THE GAME

UNKNOWN MAN

The shit you see when you're lurking in the night . . . Seemed like C was making enemies, more and more by the day. I knew it wouldn't be long before the young girl caught on. It had been nearly two years, and she was still at it. I had plenty of opportunities to do her in, but just when I was about to, she started calling again, popping shit about how much she miss a nigga. For a minute, I almost believed her. But as much as I wanted to trust the bitch, I knew she was still doing dirt. It was all game with C. I guess she hadn't gotten Snake where she wanted him, so she still needed me by her side. Sure, I was going to holla at her and hit that ass when she was giving it up, but at the same time, I was still lurking.

It was fucked up she was fucking that nigga, Duke, but I guess the bitch was so desperate to get at Snake she'd try anything. For some reason, Snake had laid off her. I wasn't really sure why, but I expected it had something to do with that stalking wifey of his, Danielle. Little did C know she had four muthafuckers hot on her trail: me, Snake, Danielle, and now that li'l chick, BJ. One false move and things could easily turn disastrous for her.

CHAPTER 20

FAMILY FUED

SNAKE

Duke just didn't get it. I was tired of talking to this li'l nigga. I didn't know what it was going to take. Every day it was a new word on the street about this nigga and the shit he was doing. Now I heard he was fucking that bitch, Ceazia. And I wouldn't be surprised if his li'l shortie knew about it too. It was all over town that one of those project chicks he was fucking caught C at his crib one night and slit their tires. Between C, the chickenheads and his li'l shortie, BJ, Duke was getting in over his head. I tried to tell that nigga Ceazia was dangerous, but he still wasn't hearing me. This was just one thing I couldn't stand back and watch. I fucked up one time by letting him move on his own, but I refused to do it again. I was going to call this li'l nigga over, so I could holla at him.

Ring, ring . . . ring, ring.

"You have reached the voicemail box of 757. . ." the recording began to say.

I didn't even bother leaving a message. I just hung up and called him on his business line. One thing for sure, that was one phone that always got answered. Duke was unquestionably 'bout the paper.

"What up, Unc?" Duke answered on the first ring.

"Yo, nigga, I need to holla at you. Come by the crib."

"A'ight, give me like an hour. I'm in the middle of something right now."

"Nah, nigga, now," I demanded, attempting to

148

put Duke in his place.

I was prepared for the usual power struggle argument, but surprisingly, Duke agreed to come right away.

"What up, sexy?"

I heard Duke greet Danielle as he walked through the door. To my surprise, Duke had arrived in less than ten minutes. I walked in the living room to see Duke lounging on the couch. He had the remote in his hand, flipping through the channels, but his attention seemed to be elsewhere. I turned my head in the direction he was looking. As soon as I turned, I knew exactly what he was admiring.

"Danielle. Go to the back. Me and Duke need to talk business," I instructed her.

"And why don't you put some clothes on while you at it?" I whispered in her ear as she headed into the bedroom.

She paused at my statement and gave me an awkward look, but dared to challenge my request. From her expression, I knew she knew exactly what I was insinuating.

My words interrupted Duke's fantasy. The constant massage of his dick as he licked his lips was a definite window into his thoughts. That li'l nigga was getting off on my girl.

"What up, li'l nigga?" I asked while flopping down on the sofa next to him and snatching the remote out of his hand. "You don't need this. You ain't paying much attention to the TV," I said sarcastically, just to let him know I saw him peeping out Danielle.

"Aw, come on, Unc. It ain't shit for me to look at Danielle. I been checking her out for the past couple of years. Don't tell me you getting all sensitive 'bout that shit now."

"Nah, man. That's the least of my worries. I'm more concerned about the shit I hear about you and C fuckin'. So, what's up with that? You knocking her off or what?" I asked sternly.

"Look, Unc. I ain't even gon' lie to you. Since she stopped fucking you, she been coming at me strong. And you know me; I ain't the one to turn down no good pussy."

It was obvious I was going to have to really break shit down to this nigga in order for him to really feel me on everything I was about to say.

"Duke, I only fucked the broad once. You ever wondered why I didn't continue fucking her after that one time?" I asked as my first attempt to bring some things to his attention.

"Nope. Not once. That ain't my concern, Unc. Evidently she wanted something different. From the looks of things, she was feeling me from the first time we met at the strip joint. The only reason she probably ain't holla is 'cause you was throwing salt in the game . . . hatin' on a nigga and shit."

Duke's comment about me hating was really burning me up, but I tried to stay focused and get my point across to his young ass. It was obvious his dick was getting a little too big for his Superman briefs. I stuck to my original point and continued the conversation.

"Duke, she's out of your league, man. The bitch

has a hidden agenda. And just so that you know, she didn't stop fucking me; I stopped fucking her. And you notice she ain't even holla at you until I dissed her trifling ass. The bitch is shiesty.

"In fact, you ain't the only nigga she started fucking after I dissed her. Word is she back fucking with that nigga, Bear. So, you think that's cool? That's probably why that nigga been giving us such a problem with business and shit lately. Look, man, the bitch is bad news and bad for business.

"And most importantly, I'm almost certain she killed Vegas. She's on her way to a death sentence. All I need is one solid piece of evidence and she's gone, Duke. I'm putting her to rest, so if for nothing else, at least drop the bitch for your uncle and my brother, Vegas," I said, putting all my cards on the table.

Duke needed to know the real. I had to open his eyes to shit, so he could know where I was coming from.

"Look, Unc. I hear everything you saying, but ain't shit popping. Vegas is dead. Let that man rest in peace. C is feeling me and I'm feeling her, so ain't shit gon' change. And as for that nigga, Bear, fuck him. He's just one man on the team. One monkey don't stop no show. As for you, all I can say is do you, Unc, 'cause I'm gon' do me without a doubt!" he said while standing up and putting on his NY cap and tilting it to the side as an indication he was leaving. "Gone!" Duke hollered then closed the front door behind him.

Shit went exactly as I expected. I knew talking

to him was like talking to a brick wall. I didn't even bother to go after Duke or force him to hear me. Fuck it. I was just gon' have to let nature take its course.

"What's going on?" Danielle asked as she walked toward the living room, now fully clothed.

"Nothing. Let's go to bed," I said, annoyed at the fact she was eavesdropping.

"Duke is having sex with Ceazia?" She continued to inquire about our conversation.

"Danielle, stop asking me about this shit. Everything's good. Now, let's go to bed," I demanded, while grabbing her by the arm and leading her toward the bedroom.

Of course Danielle wasn't letting shit go that easily. Lately, she'd become very unruly. I wasn't really sure what was causing it, but it was going to cause me to smack her ass one good time to let her know who the boss was. For some reason, she had this new attitude as if she was running shit. But in reality, she wasn't running shit here but her mouth.

Once in the bedroom, I dropped her arm and walked around her and headed to the bathroom, while she stood in the middle of the floor yelling.

"I don't want to hear this shit, Danielle," I yelled from the bathroom before closing the door.

It wasn't long before she was quiet. No one likes to argue alone. Now that shit was chill, I stepped out of the bathroom, back into the bedroom. I noticed Danielle was no longer in the room, but that was cool with me.

Relieved that the dragon was at rest, I rolled a

blunt and watched a little TV before I prepared for bed. Once I finished smoking, I glanced at the time. It was midnight, and Danielle still hadn't come to bed. I walked toward the living room to see what she was doing. It was completely dark. No lights were on, not even the television. I wondered what the fuck she was doing in the dark. I could faintly hear her speaking to someone. I walked a little closer then realized she was on the back porch. I could hear her talking, but there was no response, so I figured she was on the phone. I walked closer then stood at the door and listened.

"I don't know what's up with him, but he really needs to start treating me better before someone else steps up to the plate," I could hear her say.

Then she began to give a flirtatious laugh and stated, "Boy, you are so crazy!"

Boy? Who the fuck this bitch talking to?

I backed away and headed to the bedroom. I had to move away quickly, otherwise I would have busted through those French doors and choked the shit out of her sneaky ass. Once in the bedroom, I turned off the TV then hit speaker on the base of the cordless phone. That bitch had no idea I was listening.

"Damn, baby, I don't know why that nigga tripping. You holding shit down at home? I mean, you know, in the bedroom and shit?" I heard a familiar voice say.

"I guess. I mean, he doesn't complain."

"You don't sound confident. You deep-throatin', taking it from the back, and riding that thang too?"

"Yeah, I do all of that," Danielle said without

hesitation.

The more I listened, the angrier I became. This conversation was definitely out of line. Only curiosity kept me listening. I wanted to see just how far the two of these muthafuckers would go.

"Anybody can do those things. The question is, are you doing it right? Are you throwing that ass back when you getting hit from the back? Are you moaning with each stroke? Are you bouncing up and down on that dick, taking in every inch?"

"Mmmmmm, yeeess!" Danielle moaned as though her pussy was dripping at the thought.

"Sounds like you feeling that type of talk."

"Feeling it is not the word."

"Well, I may as well finish it up. I need you to follow my every instruction. Put your hands in your panties for me and rub that clit. Get it nice and wet for me. Once it's wet, put your fingers in your mouth and lick the juice off. Let me hear you lick those juices, baby."

"Mmmmmm, it tastes so good." Danielle forced out the words between erotic pants.

That was it. I couldn't take anymore. I threw on my clothes, grabbed my keys, and headed out the door, but before I left, I stopped by the back porch to pay Danielle a little surprise visit. I opened the door to see her with one hand on the phone, the other in her panties and her legs open on the patio table. I didn't say a word. I just looked at her. She turned around and noticed my presence, yet she didn't seem startled.

"What? Isn't this the same position you were in the day I walked in the house after getting my ass whipped by one of your bitches?" she said sarcastically then turned back around and continued her conversation. "Now, where were we, baby?"

Smack!

That was the last damn straw! Without thinking, I hauled off and smacked Danielle so hard, she dropped the phone and fell out the chair. She immediately burst into tears as though I had practically killed her. With no emotion, I walked off and closed the door behind me, locking Danielle outside.

Maybe that nigga can help her get into the house, I thought as I headed out the front door and locked it as well. It was a Sunday night, so there weren't many places to go other than the strip club and the reggae joint. Trying to avoid C, I hadn't been hitting the strip joint lately, so I chose the reggae club, The Mango Tree. Although I was not a reggae fan, I loved to watch the ladies move to that shit.

Once I got in the club, I did my usual strip club routine. I grabbed a table in the corner, near an exit. Then I hit the waitress off decent, so she could look out. As I got relaxed and sipped on my Remy, I noticed C walk in. Luckily, she didn't notice I was there. She seemed to be on another trick mission because as soon as she came in, she headed straight to this nigga from around the way. I didn't really know him, but like any nigga that's getting money, I know other niggas is getting it too. And he happened to be one of those niggas.

From what I heard, he was a Jamaican cat

down with Macten Sound that not only got it in the streets, but be killing niggas in gambling too. C and dude didn't talk very long. They had a few words and he bought her a drink. Seemed like after all her seductive tricks, she still wasn't able to get him to trick.

After her drink, C disappeared into a dark corner. I figured she posted up there to try her luck with the next nigga. I continued to enjoy my drinks and observe the many things that were going on around me. One thing I found odd is that an hour had passed and C still hadn't come out of her corner. I started to get the feeling she was trying to be inconspicuous herself. But the thing was, I wasn't really sure why.

The more I watched and thought, the more it began to make me feel a little uneasy. So, after I finished my drink, I was planning to leave. Just when I was close to leaving, I noticed Duke's li'l shortie stroll in the club, looking all Hollywood and shit.

"Damn, she sure ain't no li'l girl no more," I said to myself.

BJ was never really built as a little girl, but she had a lot of those li'l girl qualities, like the long blonde weaves, the long acrylic nails, the sneakers and the li'l girl wardrobe. I must say she had certainly stepped it up a notch. Hell, if I didn't know who she was, she would definitely be mistress material. She was young and tender, no one knew her, and I could easily mold her into whatever I wanted.

The more I stared at her, the more motivation I

had to make a move. In a matter of seconds, any thoughts of Duke were out the door.

"Fuck that nigga, Duke. He needs to see the flip side of the game. He wants to play hardball; well I'm 'bout to pitch!" I said to myself then sipped my drink, still watching BJ's every move.

I planned to make her mistress material. Duke had played his last joker card on me. I was 'bout to make that nigga really feel the wrath. I swallowed the rest of my drink in a hurry so I could meet her halfway, but before I could move, she was already headed in another direction. Ironically, she was headed toward that same Jamaican cat that C was trying to get at earlier in the night.

This nigga must really be doing it! I thought as I watched him and BJ chat away. I knew my li'l soldier was putting down for shortie, so she wasn't hurting for no money. And shit, from the way things had been looking, I thought shortie was head over heels for my li'l man. Guess she heard about that li'l incident with C after all.

I watched as she laughed and drank with dude. She seemed to really be enjoying herself, so I decided to lay off her. That was the best choice anyway. For one second, reality had begun to set in. That was Duke's girl. What the fuck was I thinking?

Hell, I knew exactly what I was thinking. I was thinking that nigga keep testing me. That nigga didn't listen. That nigga was fucking C, li'l shortie, and now on the verge of fucking my girl too. Phone sex was just the first step. I recognized the game 'cause I taught it to him. Danielle was vulnerable right now, seeking attention, trying to get a reaction out of me. What better way to do it than to feed into Duke's bullshit passes? She was falling right into the trap. He was feeding off her weak ass. If I wasn't in my right mind, I'd punish both of their sorry asses.

"Hey, Snake?" an excited voice said, interrupting my thoughts.

"Oh, damn. What's up, li'l shortie? You looking real good tonight," I said while eyeballing BJ from head to toe.

"Thank you," she said so innocently. She still had that young girl innocence, and it was turning me on.

"Would you like a drink?" I asked as I watched her dance to the reggae music.

"No thanks. I've had enough. This is my song!" she said, moving in a motion that was real familiar to me.

The more I watched, the more it registered. She moved just like that conniving bitch Ceazia. Oddly, instead of turning me off, it turned me on even more. I knew I had to make a move. She was way too innocent to accept a proposition, so I knew I had to come at her in another direction.

"Yo, I'm 'bout to get out of here. You need anything? You all right?"

"Yeah, I'm fine."

"Well, take down my number just in case something arises. You in the family since you fuck with my li'l soldier, so I gotta make sure you well taken care of."

She screwed her face up at the mention of

Duke, but without hesitation, she popped her cell phone open and took the number.

"A'ight, li'l shortie," I said before walking off.

I patted myself on the back as I headed home. It felt good to know my game was still on point. BJ feel right into the trap and gave me all the right signs. The screwed-up face was a crystal-clear sign that she wasn't feeling Duke. But I was careful not to acknowledge it, or it could be used as a motive for me to holla at her, since I knew she wasn't feeling him. Next thing I did was offer my number instead of getting hers. This still kept me in the clear, because now she had to be the aggressor. But I only did this because I was confident she would call. I knew she depended on Duke for loot, and since she wasn't feeling him, I knew she wasn't coming at him on no needy shit. The time was going to come real soon when she was going to need some money. And I specifically told her to call me if she needed anything, so when her pockets got low, I was going to be her lifeline. A guaranteed call, baby!

I pulled up to the house, reluctant to even walk in. I didn't want to be nowhere near Danielle's stupid ass. I was liable to smack the shit out of her at any moment I had a flashback. As I walked to the bedroom and saw her in bed sleeping soundly, I wondered how the fuck she'd gotten in the house. I didn't bother waking her. I just jumped in the shower, threw on some boxers and headed to the kitchen for my nightly ritual. That's when I realized exactly how she'd gotten in. That ignorant bitch threw the patio chair through the French doors. I simply shook my head in disbelief and continued with my nightly ritual.

I poured a shot of Hennessey then took a Goody's Powder to help me sleep. Since being shot, dreams had been haunting me every night. To this day, I didn't know who the shooter was at the Coliseum that day, and it still had me shook. At times, I would have liked to just rule it out and say all the bullets were meant for Ray-Ray and I just got in the crossfire, but I couldn't even think of anyone that would want that li'l nigga dead besides Duke. I'd run every possible nigga through my head, but still no one fit. Just like with Vegas's death, until that shit was figured out, I was not going to rest.

CHAPTER 21

A STAB IN THE BACK

CEAZIA

It had been several days since I'd last talked to my li'l sis, BJ. I knew she'd been through a lot with the loss of her best friend, Gina, so I'd been giving her some time to herself. But after seeing her out last night, it was apparent that she was doing just fine. Besides, I needed to know just how close she and Judah were as well as she and Snake. I wasted no time calling her up.

"Hello." BJ answered the phone in a flat tone.

"Hey, Li'l Momma! How are you?" I asked, hoping she was in the mood for chatting.

"I'm good. I'm feeling a lot better."

"I know. That's why I called. I heard you went out to The Mango Tree last night. So, how was it?" I asked in an attempt to get her to tell me some much-needed information.

"It was nice. I needed to get out the house, so I decided to go see Judah."

"Oh, so what do you think about him? Are y'all like talking or something?" I quickly began my interrogation, and she readily gave up the info.

"Well, we talk on the phone, but nothing really major. He seems like a really nice guy. I'm feeling him, and it looks like he's feeling me the same."

"Oh, okay. But what about Duke?" I asked. I threw out Duke's name in an effort to get BJ to change her feelings about Judah. Judah was my fish, and there was no way I would let BJ come in and steal my catch.

"What about him? Aren't you the one who always told me I deserve better?"

162

BJ was right. I did tell her that on a regular basis, but that was when I was trying to steal Duke from underneath her nose. I couldn't just take back all the negative things I'd said about Duke. Now my words were coming back to haunt me. How was I going to fix this one? I had to think fast, and a fast thinker I was.

"Yeah, you're right. I just don't want you rushing into anything too soon. I mean, do you even know anything about Judah?" I quizzed.

"Well, we've rapped quite a bit, and I know enough to know that he is potentially a good catch," BJ responded confidently.

From BJ's cocky response, I knew that this was going to be a task, but I planned to do all I could to change her mind about Judah. Even if I didn't convince her in one night, I knew with time I could definitely change her mind. This would only be the beginning.

I was determined to find out what BJ knew. Whatever Judah told her, I could turn it into a negative and convince her that he was not telling her the truth. Once the trust was ruined, any thoughts she had of hooking up with him would be out the door.

I could use the fact that I knew how BJ had been hurt by Duke and she didn't want to go down that same path, to my advantage. I began plotting how I could use this information to work against her if need be. I'd make her feel like she was getting herself right back into the same situation. I went forth with my dirty work.

"Well, did Judah tell you what he does for a

living?" I inquired as I began the first step toward character destruction.

"Yes, he did. He explained to me that he plays music. He has a sound in several places, and he travels to different places to play music at clubs or for different events."

"Oh, really. I guess he left out the fact that his sound is just a cover-up for what he really does," I stated, knowing BJ would inquire more.

"What do you mean, what he really does?" she asked, falling for the trap.

"He runs a huge drug ring, BJ. And those areas where he has a sound are places where he has shop set up. I know you haven't been able to tell, but Judah's a very dangerous man, BJ. Haven't you noticed how much respect he gets in the club?" I didn't let BJ respond before I continued to speak. "That's because he's a rude boy, a bad man. It's not safe to be around him. Who knows when someone is going to get the balls to step up to him and take him out? And I know you don't want to relive another death by shooting."

I hated to have to pull the death card on her, but I felt I had to come strong and hit home to convince her. BJ sat silently for a while before she responded.

"I had no idea about any of this you're telling me. You're right. Judah does get lots of respect. I noticed that from the first day we met. And no, I don't want to relive another death. I don't think I could. Maybe I'll ask him about it. He seems to be very honest. Maybe he doesn't know me well enough to tell me such things just yet."

I quickly came to realize that this little girl wasn't as naive as I had thought. I decided to take another shot at deceiving her.

"Oh, and another thing I think I should point out. Did you notice me and all my girls knew him? And did you notice he referred to me as Cinnamon?"

"Yeah, so, he's already told me he knows you all from the strip club. I have no problem with that. He's even invited me to come with him. In fact, I just may take him up on that offer and go tonight. You gon' dance tonight?" BJ asked abruptly, seemingly trying to get me off the subject of Judah.

I didn't fall for her trick. I stuck with the subject instead. "BJ . . . BJ . . . BJ. Yeah, he does know us from the strip club, but it goes a little further than that. Judah is a big gambler, and he has these card parties where he invites over strippers. And those strippers are me and my girls."

"Oh, really. So, what exactly goes on at those parties; just stripping or a little more than that?" she asked, starting to sound a little concerned.

My plan was beginning to work, so I came at BJ even stronger. "At those parties, anything goes. Unlike the strip club, there are no rules at a private party. If you got money to pay, then we play," I said in an effort to persuade her that Judah took part in these sex-escapades even though he would never leave the gambling area.

"Wow. That's a hard pill to swallow. That just really doesn't seem like Judah. I'm not going to give up on him just yet, though. I still would like to get to know him a little better. Things may not be as they seem. If they are, who knows, maybe he's willing to change for me."

I was beginning to get upset with this bitch's consistency. So, I had to go for the gusto.

"Look, BJ. I didn't want to come right out and tell you this, but he's fucking my girl, Storm, and he's been fucking her for three years now. He keeps her laced. And she's pregnant with his child as we speak."

Again the phone became silent. I was certain my last comments had gotten the best of BJ. I spoke to break the silence.

"I'm sorry, BJ. I hope you're not hurt. I tried to change your mind about him without saying that, but you just wasn't trying to hear me," I said with a phony sincerity.

"That's okay, C. Thanks for telling me. Niggas will be niggas, I guess. Well, with that news, I guess I'll call it a night and head to bed."

"Mission accomplished!" I said aloud after hanging up the phone.

I spent so much time convincing BJ to leave Judah, I didn't have time to question her about Snake. But I didn't sweat it because I knew there was going to be plenty of time for that. I sat gloating over the fact that I was knocking them out, one by one, and then thought. *Speaking of Snake, I sure could use some Jackson dick right about now. Of course, I'll have to settle for Duke since Snake is on some shit right now. But it won't be long before I have him back where I want him.*

CHUNICHI

I hit Duke on the Nextel alert.

"What's up, C?" he yelled through the speaker of the phone.

"I want to see you," I said in my most seductive tone.

"A'ight, you can come through. I'll be home in about thirty minutes."

"See you then," I said before disconnecting.

It was always simple to get whatever I wanted from Duke. The sex was pretty good for a young buck, so I didn't mind fucking him at all. Besides, every time I came over, he hit me off with some money. That was a win-win situation for me. I'd be crazy to drop that fool!

An hour later, I was at Duke's crib. I could smell the stench of Hennessey and Hypnotiq screaming from Duke's breath as he walked near me. He was obviously drunk.

"Want a drink?" The words slurred from his mouth.

"Yeah, just give me a shot of Hennessey."

I figured I'd better have something in my system, or I would be leaving soon. I would definitely need a drink just so I could tolerate Duke's drunken-ass. There was nothing worse than being sober around a drunken fool. That was one of the most irritating feelings one could have, in my opinion.

Duke brought me the Hennessey and I threw it back, taking it all in one gulp. I exhaled as the liquor burned, leaving a flaming path down my chest. Duke walked toward me, grabbed the back of my head with one hand and my ass cheek with the other, then stuck his warm tongue in my mouth, kissing me softly. This was much different from the wham-bam-thank-you-ma'am sex I was accustomed to. My body actually shivered with excitement as he kissed me passionately. Before I knew it, I was completely submissive and taken by his obsession.

Duke began to rip my clothes off piece by piece as we stumbled up the stairs toward his bedroom. Once at the top of the stairs, we busted through his bedroom doors, still indulged in passion, and landed on the dresser. He bent my naked body over and squeezed my hips tight as he inserted his penis forcefully.

"Ah! Ah! Aaaaah!" My erotic yells rang out, turning him on even more.

My body ached as Duke pounded me from the back. I continued to yell with each stroke. My ass shook and breasts bounced with each brush.

"You like that?" I could hear Duke whisper in my ear.

"Yes," I responded to a phrase that was much too familiar to me. In fact, every touch, each kiss, each stroke was all too familiar to me. Duke must have noticed my mind drifting, because he grabbed me by my hair and forced my head back.

"Whose pussy is this?" he asked while gently biting on my ear then passionately kissing me.

I looked at his reflection in the mirror. I didn't know what Duke put in that shot of Hennessy, but it really had me bugging. The image in the mirror just wasn't what I thought I should be seeing.

CHUNICHI

When I looked in the mirror, the reflection I originally saw was Duke, who then changed to Snake then to Vegas. I put my head down and closed my eyes, hoping the hallucination would disappear. Duke noticed how distracted I became, then demanded my attention.

"Whose pussy is this?" Duke asked again, pulling my hair, forcing me to look in the mirror once again.

"It's yours, Duke. It's yours." I closed my eyes and forced the words out my mouth.

"Open your eyes and look in the mirror. Watch me fuck my pussy then, bitch!"

I slowly opened my eyes and looked at the mirror, this time focusing on my reflection. That's when the truth settled. While watching the image of me in the mirror, I realized everything I really wanted at that moment. The touch I'd felt were the hands of Vegas, the kiss I'd felt were the lips of Vegas, and the passion I'd felt was the hunger of Vegas. This took me back to the memorable moments of the sweet love Vegas and I shared. Vegas and I used to make love like we were all that mattered to each other. Like my life before my eyes, each scene flashed before me in the mirror.

The memory of our anniversary night on the cruise was vivid. I could almost feel the cool air around me as I thought of Vegas secretly sexing me from behind in the night air. Then there was the spontaneous moment we shared together on the weight bench in our home.

"Whose pussy is this?" Duke asked again, interrupting my thoughts like a flick of the remote.

MARRIED TO THE GAME

My mind was now on Snake. The familiar words "You like that? Whose pussy is this?" were the words of Snake. I thought of the rough sex we'd shared at the hotel. As I thought back to the multitude of bruises I had the next day, I could only wonder why the sex we shared was so different from the passionate lovemaking I was quite sure he'd made with Mickie, time and time again. As I looked in the mirror and stared into the eyes of the young Duke, it was apparent that these three men shared something a little more powerful than a last name. It was an uncontrollable attraction that brewed a combined lust I had for each of them.

CHAPTER 22

HAVE MY CAKE AND EAT IT TOO

DUKE

Who the fuck said you can't have your cake and eat it too? Well, somebody needed to pass the word to the muthafucker that li'l Duke from Norfolk, Virginia made history! Not only did I have the cake and eat it, but I did it while everyone was watching. I was just that sweet! Just to boost my ego, I thought I'd give that shit a try right now. I'd already had C and ran her ass. Now I'd call Danielle. She was going to be my next piece of booty. Things with her were moving easier than expected.

I picked up the phone and pressed *67 before dialing her cell number.

"What's up, Duke?" she asked before even saying hello.

"And how did you know it was me, sexy?"

"No one else blocks their number when calling, except you," she stated in a flirtatious tone.

My manhood rose at the sound of her voice. I had to get her and fast.

"So, how you doing?" I asked, knowing that she would likely mention some drama that she and Snake were going through.

"Not too good, Duke. Not too good," she stated sadly.

"What's wrong, baby girl?"

"It's Snake. He just won't treat me right. I know I was wrong for that little escapade that you and I had, but compared to the things he's done, that's nothing. I've never cheated or even looked at another guy. That conversation between us wasn't even supposed to happen. He won't forgive me. I don't know what to do. Do you think you could talk to him?" Her words were music to my ears.

Now that Snake was mad at her, it made her even more vulnerable, which made things easier for me. All I had to do now was act like I was there for her.

"To be honest, Danielle, Snake is not even feeling me right now. Me and that nigga ain't really getting along," I said, hoping that she would inquire more about things between my uncle and me.

"What do you mean? Is it because he caught us on the phone that night?"

"Nah, actually I haven't even spoken to him about that. He was pissed off at me before that. He was mad from when I left your house earlier that night."

"So, what happened? I heard you all speaking about that girl, Ceazia. Does it have anything to do with her?" Danielle was falling into each one of my traps perfectly.

"Yeah, it did. But I'd rather not go into it," I said to draw more curiosity.

"Duke, please tell me what's going on. It must be something really bad to tear you guys apart. I mean, you all were like father and son." Danielle begged to hear more, and I quickly gave her an earful.

"Danielle, even though Snake and I have our differences, he's still my uncle, and I have to be loyal to him. But at the same time, I got much love for you, so I'm just going to leave it at this. You're a good girl and you deserve a good man. Any nigga would love to have a woman like you, so you don't have to settle. You see all the signs. I don't have to point shit out to you. I know you've heard the saying 'if it looks like a duck and quacks like a duck, then it's a duck.' Well, in this case, let's just say; if it looks like a stripper, and acts like a gold-digging ho, then it's Ceazia," I said, wrapping shit up perfectly.

"I know exactly what you're saying, Duke. You don't have to say anything more. On that note, I think I'll say goodnight."

"Good night, sweetie. And if you need to talk, don't hesitate to call. I'll hop out the best pussy to talk to you," I said with a chuckle to add icing to the cake.

I knew it wouldn't be long before I had Danielle screaming my name like the rest. It was only a matter of time. I had to move slowly with her, but with Snake's assistance, things were moving right along. His fucked up attitude was pushing his girl into my arms.

So, that was two down, now one to go. I wanted to taste a piece of BJ's cake now. Since her girl died, she'd been real fucked up, so I'd been chilling. But I thought she'd had enough time to heal. Even more importantly, I was starting to miss that tight poonanny. BJ was definitely a prize possession. I broke her virginity, so I owned the pussy, and I planned to keep it that way.

Ring . . . ring . . . ring . . . ring . . . ring . . . ring.

"You have reached . . ." the automated voicemail began to say.

That was odd because it was late, and I knew BJ wasn't out anywhere. I decided to try calling again.

"Hello?" This time, she answered on the second ring.

"Why the fuck you ain't answer the phone when I just called? How many times do I have to call to get an answer?" I yelled.

"Why the fuck is you calling me with this bullshit?" she yelled back then hung the phone up in my ear.

That shit really fucked me up.

Where the fuck did she get balls to one, talk to me like that and two, to hang up the phone on me? I thought as I dialed her number again. I figured that death shit must have really got her tripping.

"Hel-lo?" she answered in an annoyed tone.

"What's up, baby? How you feel?" This time I tried a different approach. My goal was to fuck not fight, so I figured I'd better chill out.

"I'm good, Duke. What do you want?"

"Whatchu mean? I'm calling to talk to my girl. You are my girl, aren't you?"

"The last I checked, although you don't act like it. A real boyfriend would have sent flowers, dropped by for a surprise visit, called constantly. You, on the other hand, just dropped off the face of the earth."

She was right. There wasn't much I could say. During the time BJ was mourning, I was using it as an opportunity to fuck C and any other broad willing to give up some ass. But even though she was right, I refused to admit it. I had to come up with something.

"I'm sorry, baby. I've never had to console someone during a loss, so I don't know how to act. Please forgive me. As a matter of fact, why don't you let me make it up to you?" I began to run game on her.

"Make it up to me, huh? And just how do you plan to do that?" she asked.

"How about this? Just throw on some clothes and come over right now."

"No, Duke, I don't think that's a good idea." She declined my offer.

"Why not, baby? I miss you. I miss seeing that sexy body, I miss your pretty smile, I miss holding you at night, and most importantly, I miss you farting in your sleep."

She laughed hysterically.

"See, I bet you haven't laughed that hard in days. Who else besides me can do such a thing?"

"You're right, Duke. I think I'll take you up on that offer. You better make it worth my while too, nigga!" BJ stated before hanging up the phone.

I rushed and filled the bathtub with hot water. I added BJ's favorite bath beads from Bath and Body Works and lit candles all around the tub. Then I ran to the kitchen and grabbed some strawberries, cherries, and grapes. These were all BJ's favorite fruits. As a final touch, I ran to the corner store and grabbed a single rose and a cheesy little card that simply read "I love you."

The killer would be the message I wrote inside. Nothing makes a woman's heart melt faster than shit from the heart. A woman would appreciate a blank card with a handwritten message from the heart more than a Hallmark card with a beautiful poem. I reached into my box of cards, letters, pictures and many items I'd collected from women over the past years. I grabbed a letter from my ex-girlfriend, Kim Todd. Her poems always said the right things. I figured I'd change a few words to make it fit, and put that same poem in my card to BJ. I knew this box of love would come in handy for something other than a booty call one day.

Once I finished writing, I ran to the bed and placed the rose and card on it, and set some vanilla massage oil on the nightstand. Then I grabbed my *Love and Basketball* DVD and put it in the player. That was her favorite movie, and I knew she would want to watch it.

A good twenty minutes hadn't passed before my doorbell rang. I was sure to turn all phones off, both house and cell, before opening the door. I wasn't taking no chances in fucking this up. Hell, even I knew there were some situations not even the tightest game could fix.

"Hey baby!" I said before kissing BJ on the cheek.

She greeted me with a tight hug. And surprisingly, I was really feeling it. I stepped back and looked at her as she headed to the bedroom. For a moment, I felt as though I was lucky to have her. But I quickly shook it off and guided her to the bathroom.

"I have a hot bath waiting for you with your favorite bath beads. Why don't you get in and I'll bathe you?" I suggested.

"This is nice, Duke. I didn't know you had it in you," she said, surprised by my actions.

"Anything for my baby," I said seductively, then smiled and licked my lips.

I grabbed the net sponge and filled it with body wash. I started with her toes and washed each one gently, then slowly moved up, washing each part of her body, while complimenting and giving each a gentle kiss. She melted with each kiss. After her bath, I led her to the bed and directed her to lie down. I poured vanilla massage oil all over her body then I gave her the massage of a lifetime. She moaned and the tension from her body lifted with my tender touch. When I was done, she was so relaxed. As she lay on her back, I pressed play to begin the movie then fed her fruit as we watched. When the movie was done, she looked at me mysteriously and stated, "Duke, what has come over you? What more could a woman ask for?"

And with that said, I responded, "Just one more thing." Then I handed her the rose and card.

Tears welled up in her eyes as she read the words of the card aloud: "My love, my heart, I have loved you from the start. Please forgive my doggish ways, for it is with you I want to stay. I can't live without you—no, I shall not. Please come back home, I love you a lot. Love always, Duke."

When she was done, she gave me a passionate kiss and stroked my erect penis.

Thanks, Kim! I said to myself, anticipating what was to come next. I knew after reading the card, this kiss could only lead to hot, wild, passionate sex, but I grabbed her hand and refused.

"No, baby. Tonight is all about you," I whispered softly in her ear.

Then I lay her on her back and kissed each part of her body before resting my head in her lap and sending her into ecstasy.

CHAPTER 23

REVENGE TASTES LIKE CHOCOLATE

BJ

Damn, you really put it on me, I thought as I stared at a peacefully sleeping Duke. I wondered how he did the things he did then just acted like nothing had ever happened when he was around me. If I didn't know any better, I would think this nigga was truly in love. It was sad, but hell, the more I looked at him, the more I realized I was still in love. Although I knew about the dirt he'd done, I still desired to be with him. We'd been through so much together. How could I possibly just walk away? I mean, this was the man I lost my virginity to. I'd never made love to anyone besides him. I didn't even know if I was capable of making love with anyone else.

"I love you, Duke," I whispered softly then kissed his cheeks.

I rubbed my hand across his scarred chest. Tears came in my eyes as I thought back to the day of the shooting. I almost lost him to war and now I was losing him to lust, after all I'd sacrificed. I lost my best friend, Gina, because of Duke. I lost my cousin, Ray-Ray, because of Duke. And more importantly, I lost my purity to Duke. And how did he repay me? By sleeping with a girl he knew I considered a big sister. How could I just sit and let shit ride? I couldn't do it. I refused to do it. No matter how much I loved him; that love wasn't going to make up for all my losses. That was it; I'd made my mind up. I should have never come here in the first place.

I hopped out of the bed and began putting my clothes on in a hurry. I didn't want to take the chance of waking Duke. If he woke up, it would be even harder for me to walk away. Before I left, I stopped in the kitchen and wrote a small message on a notepad. It read: *Sorry but I can no longer do this. It is over, Duke. Love always, BJ*

I knew that was cheesy, but it was the only way I could do it. There was no way I would be able to face him straight-up. I took one last deep breath then placed the note underneath the refrigerator magnet, walked out the door and said good-bye forever.

The ride home was long, even though I only lived ten minutes away. I wondered if I'd made the right choice. My heart was telling me no, but my mind was telling me yes. Once I got home, the thought of Duke began to haunt me once again. I had to do something to get him off my mind. So, in a desperate attempt to get him out of my thoughts, I called Judah.

"Yo?" I heard the comforting baritone voice.

"Hey, Judah. How are you?"

"I'm good. How are you?" he asked.

I was relieved he'd asked because there was a lot I wanted to share. I wasn't sure where to start, so I figured I'd bring up Ceazia and see where the conversation went.

"I'm okay, I guess. Just got a lot on my mind."

"Oh, yeah? Like what?" he curiously asked.

"Nothing big. For starters, I just need to ask you a few questions. I spoke to Ceazia the other day and—"

"Ceazia? Please don't tell me that trifling bitch feeding you bullshit." Judah interrupted.

"Well, she told me some things that I just want to ask you about. Let's start with these parties that you have. Do you engage in sex with any of the strippers there?" I nervously asked while praying he'd give the right answer.

"No, I don't. Those parties are mostly about gambling. I just invite the girls to lure in more guys. I watch the table all night, baby."

"Well, what about other than the parties. Did you ever have sex with any of them?"

"Look, BJ, from the day you met me, I've been nothing but honest to you, and that's not going to change. So, if you ask me a question, just be sure you want to know the answer," he stated as though he was preparing me for bad news.

"I want to know, Judah. I don't want to come into this relationship blind. Let me know what I may have to face in the future."

"Okay, look. I did have sex with one of the girls on a regular basis. It was nothing serious, just something to pass time. The girl would always want to include Cinnamon, or Ceazia as you call her, in our sexual escapades. I was never really feeling Cinnamon, so I would decline. I would watch them, but I only had sex with her friend. After a while, I stopped dealing with the chick, and she started acting all crazy and shit. Now she claims she's pregnant. When we were together, I would look out for her very generously and even look out for Cinnamon too. So, now that I'm gone, the money is gone. And now that they see I'm feeling you, they're doing all they can to fuck shit up. So, it's up to you, baby girl. You can stick with me and believe what I tell you, or listen to them and give them what they want."

After listening to Judah, I believed him. I'd heard the tales and even learned from firsthand experience that C was a conniving little bitch and would do anything to get on top. She may have gotten Duke, but I'd be damned if she got Judah!

"Don't worry, Judah. I believe everything you're saying. Trust me, I know how Ceazia gets down. I got your back as long as you got mine, baby," I said, confident that I'd made the right decision.

"Good to go?"

"Excuse me?" I said, confused by his Jamaican slang.

"Everything straight?" he stated in between laughs at my ignorance.

"Oh yeah, everything good to go."

"We're gonna have to work on your patois I see. Lata."

"Bye." I felt relieved as I hung up the phone.

It felt so refreshing to talk with Judah. It was like he was my sunray during the storm. Every time I was down, I could count on him to lift me up.

As I prepared a hot bath and got my clothes out for the day, I thought of that bitch, C. I owed her, and I owed her big time. I had to get revenge, but it had to be sweet. It had to be something that would make that bitch think twice the next time she did some fucked up shit.

While in the tub, I thought long and hard, but I couldn't think of anything. I figured I'd have to start hanging out with her more. I needed to find out her deepest secrets then use them to destroy her. Once I got out of the tub, I was ready to begin my journey to the sweetest revenge. I called her up.

"Hey, big sis!" I said full of fake enthusiasm.

"What's up, Li'l Momma? You sound much better," she responded in a tone that I was sure was just as fake as my own.

"Nothing, just ready to get out the house and do some things; go shopping, get my nails and hair done, you know, girl stuff."

"Okay, well, you know I'm always down for a girl's day out, so why don't I come by and scoop you and we can go out together?" she offered.

Normally, I would be skeptical, but this time I had my own agenda, so I readily accepted her offer.

"Okay, come by in an hour."

"Cool. See ya then," she stated then hung up the phone.

Once I hung up, I realized I didn't have any money for a girl's day out.

"Let me think . . . let me think . . . Judah! Nah, I can't call him for money already. Duke! Nah, just left him a Dear John letter."

I had no one to call. I grabbed my purse to see just how much money I had. Then it hit me. Snake! He said if I ever needed anything to just call. Well, I needed something, and I needed it fast. I wasted no time calling him up.

"Hello?" a deep voice said from the other end of the phone.

"Hi, Snake. This is BJ," I said timidly.

"Oh, shit. What up, li'l shortie?" He seemed excited to hear from me.

"Well, I called because you said to call if I needed anything. I'm sorta in a bind. Do you think you could help me out?" I forced the words out.

"No problem. Just come check me. I'm in the area right now. Meet me at the barber shop on Granby. You know the spot."

"Okay, I'm on my way," I said before hanging up the phone.

"Thank God for that nigga," I said aloud as I grabbed my purse and headed out the door.

The barber shop was only around the corner, so it took me no time to get there. I parked my car right in front and took my time strutting up to the door. All eyes were on me as I pranced inside to the barber chair.

"Damn, li'l shortie, that was fast," Snake said, surprised that I'd arrived so quickly.

"Oh, I was already on my way out when I called," I lied, trying to make it seem like I wasn't as desperate as I looked.

"Right, right," he said while digging in his pocket then handing me a wad of money.

I didn't bother to count it. I thought that would be quite tacky.

"Thank you. I really appreciate it," I said then gave him a tight hug and little flirtatious look.

"Anytime, sweetie," he responded as I rushed out.

Now back to the crib to wait for shiesty C's arrival. So far everything had fallen right in place and I hoped my day with her would go just as smoothly.

CHUNICHI

I could hear the horn of C's 745 from my upstairs window. Like always, she was right on time. I put on my phony face, grabbed my Marc Jacob bag, and once again ran out the front door.

"Hey, girl!" I yelled while waving my hand in the air.

"What's up, Li'l Momma?" she asked while opening the passenger door from the inside of the car. She seemed pretty happy to see me. I figured she was better at being fake than anyone, but when you're as devious as that bitch I guess you have to be that way.

"So, what's on the agenda for today?" I asked as I plopped down on the leather seat and put on my seatbelt.

"Well, we can start by grabbing lunch then we'll head to the spa then to the mall. How does that sound?"

She'd said exactly what I wanted to hear. That would give us the perfect opportunity to chat and hopefully pull some skeletons out of the closet.

"Sounds good," I quickly agreed.

Ceazia picked my favorite spot: The Cheesecake Factory. Once we were seated, I quickly started the chat circle. So that I didn't seem too obvious, I started the conversation by talking about my problems. I knew that was all it took to get that girl to talking. From previous conversation, I'd learned that stories about men mistreating women really burned her up. At times, she would get so upset that you'd think she was the one actually involved. So, I began the conversation by telling her how depressed I'd been the past couple of weeks because of Gina's death and because of issues with Duke. Of course, she was more concerned with the issues I had with Duke, and she encouraged me to elaborate. And that I did—elaborate and exaggerate!

With tears in my eyes, I spoke. "I feel like Duke doesn't appreciate me. He treats me like shit. I've been nothing but good to this guy, C. Why can't he treat me right?" I begged her for the answer.

"BJ, like I've told you many times before, the answer is simple. You are too good for him," she stated as though that was the answer to all my problems.

"I understand what you're saying, C, but it's not that simple. I just can't tell myself I'm too good and walk away. Duke is the only thing I have. I've lost the two other people that were close to me. Gina is gone and Ray-Ray is gone. And the sad part about it is the reason the both of them are gone is because of Duke. He took them away from me. Hell, he's even taken my virginity. I've given so much to keep this guy happy. All I ask in return is that he does the same."

"Well, what exactly is he doing? Whatever it is, it must not be that bad because it's not enough to make you leave him," C inquired.

"Well, I found out that he's cheating on me. I'm not really sure with who, but I know for a fact he is. I really don't want to get into it because it makes me so mad. I mean to the point like, if I find out who it is, I may just do something crazy."

"Umph! I know what you mean, girl. Niggas will make you snap and lose your mind. It seems like

Duke just can't help himself, Li'l Momma. It's in his blood. All those damn Jackson men are alike. God cursed the man that made them."

"Well, why you say that? From what I hear on the streets, you had the good life when Duke's Uncle Vegas was alive. I hear he loved you to death and did everything for you," I stated, hoping Ceazia would elaborate.

I knew from the animosity she had toward men and the constant warnings Duke would give me about her, that something terrible had to have happened with her and Vegas.

"Yeah, he did. But things aren't always as they seem. You see, a guy can do and say anything, but the true test is what goes on when you're not watching. Trust me, honey, everything between me and Vegas wasn't always peaches and cream. As a matter of fact, just like you, I've made a hell of a lot of sacrifices for that man. You'd be surprised at the things I did for him." C's face became saddened and she put her head down.

I was sure I'd hit a soft spot. I'd never seen the strong, spirited, "fuck niggas and get money" Ceazia so distressed. I kept the conversation going in hopes she'd tell me more.

"So, what did he do that was so bad?"

"The ultimate, BJ. The ultimate," she stated while shaking her head left and right.

"Well, like you told me, it must have not been that bad because you didn't leave him," I said sarcastically.

"And how would you know?" Ceazia responded in an angry tone. Obviously my statement had offended her.

"Well, because you all were together until his death. If you had left him, y'all would not have been together when he died."

My cell phone rang, interrupting our conversation. I glanced down at the caller ID and it read: SNAKE.

I wondered what he wanted but I couldn't risk losing this conversation, so I hit the end button on top of the phone and sent him to voicemail.

"Sorry about that. Now, where were we?"

"We were at the part where you assumed that I did not have the strength to leave Vegas after he'd deceived me in the most tormenting way."

"Oh yeah. So, what did he do and how did you handle it?" I asked.

"I really don't want to get into it, Li'l Momma. But just know that I handled mine, and now you need to get the strength to handle yours. Hopefully, one day Snake's little princess will get some strength and handle hers too."

"C, I hope you don't get upset when I say this, but it seems to me that you have some sort of vendetta against any and every Jackson man," I stated in an attempt to get the story out.

"Vendetta? That would be too nice of a word. I despise those muthafuckers, and I'm justified to feel that way." The more Ceazia spoke the angrier she became.

"Well, maybe if you explained things to me, it would give me strength. I'm sorry, but right now I

CHUNICHI

just can't sympathize with you. You have to explain to me why you're so angry."

Ceazia took a deep breath and slowly exhaled. She scooted over closer to me in the booth then grabbed my hand and looked me in the eyes.

"BJ, what I'm about to tell you I have never shared with anyone. But like I've said many times before, I consider you my little sister, so I'd trust you with my life. And that's the only reason I'm telling you this."

"I understand, C. Your secret is safe with me," I assured her.

"Okay. After serving time in jail for a crime involving Vegas, I was released and came home unannounced to surprise him. Well, I ended up being the one surprised. I walked in on Vegas, my best friend, and another female in the Jacuzzi getting high and making out." Ceazia paused to wipe the tears that were streaming down her cheeks then she continued. "BJ, I was numb with hurt when I saw that. I literally blacked out. It was as though I was in a trance as I shot continuously into the tub, killing Vegas and his two counterparts."

My mouth dropped with disbelief. I was speechless. I had no idea how to respond, so I just did what came naturally. I grabbed her and hugged her.

"I'm sorry, C. I had no idea. I am really sorry," I said sincerely.

How could I ever deceive this girl? She can't help her actions. She's been burned so baldly it's ruined her completely. Her concept of trust, love, and even

191

her ability to have a stable relationship has been ruined, I thought as I consoled her. I had a total change of heart. I had no idea Ceazia was so disturbed.

As we finished eating, C continued to tell me about the realness behind the relationship that she and Vegas had. As we enjoyed our day at the spa and shopped, she continued to share. By the time I reached home that night, Ceazia had nearly shared her entire life story with me. My heart really went out to her. She had been from extreme highs to extreme lows. The poor girl just wanted that life she'd always dreamed of. After a day with her, I was much more appreciative for my life. I guess what they say is true: Things aren't always what they seem.

CHAPTER 24

A WOMAN'S INTUITION

DANIELLE

It was midnight, and another night that Snake's ass wasn't home. I'd had it with Snake and his bullshit. Duke was right; I was too good for Snake's cheating ass. It was sad when a young kid like Duke could recognize a good woman before a grown-ass man. But that's okay, because if Snake wouldn't love me, there were many men out there who would. And to bring that to his attention, I was going to feed into every little pass his little soldier made at me. Hell, from that phone sex he gave me the other night, Duke didn't seem so little after all.

I was going to do everything I could to catch Snake's ass out there, and as soon as it happened, I was gone. Sure, he took care of home, but he was not doing anything that the next man couldn't do.

Ring . . . ring.

How amazing, it was Snake calling. *Let's see what lie he has tonight.*

"Hello?"

"What up?" he asked as though it was six in the evening and not past midnight.

"Nothing is up, Snake. What do you want?" I asked in an annoyed tone.

"Look, Danielle, I'm really upset right now. I was actually calling because I feel real fucked up and I needed someone to talk to, but I see you're not that person."

Click!

Snake hung up on me. I was taken by surprise. I didn't know how to react—not because he hung up in my ear, because that was the norm, but I was baffled by his tone. Snake really did seem upset. There was really something wrong with him. Everything began to run through my mind.

Maybe it's Duke. Maybe he's hurt again. Duke and Snake were just talking about some rumors on the streets. Or maybe Snake's in trouble. Maybe he got robbed or arrested. Oh my God! I have to call back.

I got myself together then struggled to call Snake back. His phone went straight to voicemail. I dialed the number over and over again. Before I knew it, I'd dialed his number over twenty times and it was still going to voicemail. Then I tried text messaging him. Still no response. I didn't know what to do next. Then it hit me—Duke! I could call Duke. I figured he would know if there was a problem before anyone.

"Duke!" I yelled into the phone in a panic as soon as he picked up.

"What's up, Danielle? What's wrong, baby?" he asked, concerned.

"It's Snake. Where is he? He called and he was really upset. Now his phone is off. I think something is wrong. Have you talked to him?" I spat a thousand questions at him at once.

"Slow down, momma. Slow down. I'm sure Snake is a'ight. He would have called me if some shit went down. Just chill out. I'm gonna check on shit for you and let you know what's up."

"Okay, Duke," I reluctantly agreed before hanging up.

I felt little reassurance after speaking with Duke. I was still afraid something had gone wrong with Snake. I paced the floor back and forth while waiting to hear from Duke. After an hour passed and still no return call, I began to dial Snake's number again. And just as before, it went straight to voicemail. I could no longer wait for Duke to call me back. An hour was long enough. I grabbed the cordless phone and dialed his number.

"Yeah, Danielle," he said as soon as he picked up.

"Did you hear from him?" I eagerly asked.

"Nah, but I checked shit out and everybody that saw him out the way say he's been fine all day, so everything's cool. Just try to get some rest. I'm sure he'll be home soon."

"Okay, Duke," I reluctantly agreed just as before and hung up.

Again, I found myself pacing the floor. I had to do something to get some rest, so I took a couple of sleeping pills and lay down. I tossed and turned for another hour. It wasn't happening. I couldn't think about anything except Snake. That was it. I'd made up my mind. If Duke wouldn't look for Snake, then I would. I hopped out of bed and got dressed. I called Snake's phone one final time. Just as all the times before, it went straight to his voicemail. I grabbed my purse, dropped in the gun Snake had given me for emergencies, and headed out the door. My first stop was Park Place in Norfolk. That was where Snake spent most of his time. I drove by the barber shop, and it was closed. Not a person in sight, not even one person on the block. Then I rode past his family's house a few blocks away, and there were no signs of Snake there. There was only one other place to check—the strip club. So, that's where I headed. And lo and behold, that was where I found him.

My first instinct was to run in the club and smack the shit out of him just for making me worry. But I soon snapped back to reality, which was an ass-beatin' out of this world if I was to ever embarrass Snake in public. Now, in my right state of mind, I began to think of a plan. As I was sitting, Duke drove up. I wondered what the hell was so intriguing about a damn strip club to make these men so devoted to coming every night. I continued to sit in my car, thinking of a master plan, when my phone rang. It was Duke.

I guess he is a man of his word, I thought, assuming he was calling to tell me Snake was okay.

"Hello?" I answered on the first ring.

"I was calling to check on you," Duke stated.

"Oh, I'm fine."

"A'ight. Well, hit me if you need anything." Duke began to wrap up the conversation.

"Well, have you heard from Snake?" I asked, curious to see how Duke would respond.

"Nah, but trust me, he a'ight."

"Okay. Well, I'm going to bed," I lied then hung up. I wasn't really sure why Duke lied to me, but I was determined to find out. I'd always considered him an ally, but now I saw him as mole.

I waited for Duke to enter the club then I threw my car in drive and sped out of the parking lot.

The entire drive home, my mind raced. I couldn't believe both Duke and Snake would attempt to pull wool over my eyes. But little did they both know, I would get to the bottom of this shit.

I pulled into the driveway and raced in the house. The first place I headed was the bedroom. I'd never been the one to look for trouble because I was always taught that if you look, you shall find, but this time Snake had pushed me there. I began my search in his nightstand drawer. There I found several napkins with females' names on them and phone numbers. From the sound of the names, it wouldn't take a genius to figure out these were numbers he'd collected from the damn strip club. As I searched further, I came across a piece of paper that had the name Ceazia written in Snake's handwriting, with several phone numbers and an address.

"Ceazia . . . Ceazia." I repeated the name aloud.

That name seemed familiar to me, but I just couldn't put my finger on it. For the moment, I put that in the back of my mind as I continued to investigate. I went to his closet and began to look around. Snake and I had separate closets, so other than hanging his clothes from the dry cleaners, I never explored his closet. But one thing I did know was he kept his personal weed stash in there and he also kept a box where he threw dollar bills and coins. So, those were the two places I checked. I started with the weed stash and I found nothing. Then I came across the money box. I searched there. That's when I came across a nude photo. It was actually set up as a model's comp card. There was a large photo on one side in black and white, and several smaller photos on the other side in color. It had a name and contact numbers listed underneath. The name read Cinnamon. The bitch was obviously a stripper.

I examined the card thoroughly, looking at each picture. As I looked at the photos, the chick began to seem familiar to me. Again, I couldn't really put my finger on it. I didn't know if the sleeping pills were starting to kick in or what, but for some reason, I just couldn't think. I figured I was just too anxious.

The few things I found were enough to prove Snake was up to something, but I just needed time to bring it all together. I grabbed the photo and paper with the information on it and headed to my office in the house to make a quick copy and return the originals to their secret spots. As I made the copies things began to come together. The girl on the photo was that bitch from the hospital. I knew she was a stripper from the time I met her.

So Cinnamon is her name, huh?

Then I went on to make a copy of the paper with the name Ceazia and phone numbers. That's when I noticed the number on that paper matched the number on the photo.

"Well, I'll be damned!" I said out loud.

Shit had finally come together. The bitch from the hospital was Ceazia, Vegas' ex-girlfriend. No wonder when she was beginning to explain to me who she was, Snake stopped her. I'd heard the stories about Ceazia, but I never saw her. So she was a stripper! I couldn't believe Snake would stoop so low as to fuck with his deceased brother's girlfriend. That muthafucker! And to think I had all of that little bitch's life in the palms of my hand—literally. Revenge is a bitch, and all I have to say is Ceazia, Duke, and Snake all had better watch out!

CHAPTER 25

SMILING DECEIT

SNAKE

That sneaky bitch had no idea what she had coming to her. I knew the day would come, and it was finally here.

Look at her dancing and flaunting as though she's got every nigga hypnotized. One thang fo' sho' is I am one nigga that's broken from her trance. Those days are long gone.

Too bad that li'l nigga Duke was all caught up. It was a damn shame. He was lined up at the stage just like the rest of them cats, blind to that bitch's wicked ways. But just like the Wicked Witch of the West, that evil bitch had to go. And I was going to be the one to make sure that happened.

"What up, sexy boy?" Ceazia said as she hopped off the stage.

This was exactly what I needed. She was making shit easier than I expected.

"What up, sexy girl?" I responded while looking her up and down.

Ceazia came to an abrupt halt.

"Excuse me? You're actually responding to me?" she stated, surprised by my pleasant demeanor.

"Yeah, is something wrong with that?" I continued, trying to completely play my part.

"Lately you've been giving me a serious cold shoulder, so I thought we were on some beef shit."

"Nah, I just been having some problems at home, and a lot of shit going on in the streets, so I've been on some ill shit lately. Nothing directed toward you personally, though," I lied.

And just like that, C began her flirt routine. As she chatted with me and rubbed her hands across my face and through my hair, I noticed Duke staring from across the club. I began to tune Ceazia out as I read Duke's actions. He was obviously upset about the conversation that C and I were having. Knowing Duke, he was thinking I told him to stop hollering at her so I could holla. I bet that li'l ignorant nigga wasn't even thinking about what I told him the other day about knocking C off. After a few more minutes of talking, Duke had finally either gotten angry enough or gotten the balls to confront me about C.

"What up, Snake?" Duke said, calling me by my name instead of the usual "Unc."

"What up, Li'l Soldier." I responded as a reminder that he was still training to be where I was.

"I'm surprised to see you talking to C. From our last conversation, I thought you weren't feeling her at all," Duke said, attempting to call me out in front of Ceazia.

"Me and C already had that convo. Right, baby girl?" I stated while stroking the small of Ceazia's back.

"Yep!" she quickly responded, full of smiles.

It was so simple to get her where I wanted her. Not happy with the way things were going, Duke grabbed C by the arm and pulled her away, yelling, "I need to talk to you."

Like a rag doll, he jerked her around while yelling profanity. That whole scene was pretty comical to me. It was amazing the power a cat could have over a chick, just because he was feeding her a few dollars every now and then. After Duke finished scolding Ceazia as though she was a young child, it was my turn. I walked up to him and said the same.

"Yo, we need to talk," I whispered in his ear.

Amazingly, he didn't put up a fight. Duke followed as I walked out the club and headed to the truck. Before I could say anything, he began to speak.

"What up with you and C, man?"

"Ain't shit, Duke. Like I told you, once it was confirmed she killed Vegas, I was taking her out." I tried explaining things to Duke.

"Man, I wish you would get off that shit. If homicide investigators can't pin her to the murder, what makes you think you can?"

"Look, Duke, I have all the evidence I need. You either down with me or you're not." I couldn't tell Duke how I'd gotten the evidence because I didn't want to put nobody, including myself, in the hot-seat.

"Whateva, man. Like I said before, do you and I'm gon' do me. Enough talking," Duke said before hopping out of the truck.

I knew this wasn't gonna go easy, but I just couldn't tell Duke all the details. I wasn't trying to incriminate his li'l shortie, BJ. Nor was I trying to self-incriminate. Hell, on the real, I don't even think BJ realized she was the leak. It all happened by chance. All I could say was old Vegas must have been looking down on me.

CHUNICHI

Earlier that day, I called BJ to make sure she was straight with the little change I'd given her to handle some things. I assumed that when I called, she was in the middle of a serious conversation with Ceazia, so she attempted to send me to voicemail. Instead, she mistakenly pressed the speaker button, allowing me to hear the entire conversation, which ended up turning into a detailed confession of Ceazia killing Vegas. I had a ton of mixed emotions as I listened to them talk. At times I felt angry, then sad, then responsible. My stomach ached as each word Ceazia spoke pierced my heart.

After hearing that confession, I was ready to kill her at first sight, but I knew I had to remain calm to execute the perfect plan. So after a few shots of Hennessey and a blunt filled with purple haze, I was relaxed enough to devise the perfect plan.

I'd already taken the first steps at the club. Now I just needed to secure my position. An unexpected phone call would do the trick.

Ring . . . ring . . . ring.

I called Ceazia from my truck parked outside the club.

"Hey, sexy," Ceazia sang into the phone.

"What up. I need some companionship. I can't think of anyone I'd rather be with right now, other than you. What you gon' do about that?"

"Whatever you want, baby. You already know how I feel. I'm always down for being with a real one like you. What, your girl not turning the tricks I turn?" she asked seductively.

"Nah, she holding shit down, but I just want something different," I lied. "If you think you can fit the bill, then I need you to come roll with me."

"Fit the bill? I can be all you need and then some. I just feel sorry for your girl 'cause after tonight, I'll be all the woman you can ever think of," Ceazia said convincingly.

Shit, she actually began to turn me on. The truth is, I hadn't had sex with Danielle in over a week. Before she refused to touch me because she was certain I was cheating. Now, the tables had turned, and I wouldn't want Danielle to touch me with a ten-foot pole. If she got any closer than that, I was liable to smack her back in time. I needed a bitch to turn some tricks—not necessarily Ceazia, though. At this point, any bitch would do. But since I had a scheme going, trying to work on some shit with C, I figured I may as well take advantage of the situation. I continued to listen and rapped noise to her.

"Yeah, sexy, you sounding just like the something different I've been waiting on," I flirted.

"Well, yeah, I'm that something different, but I have to be totally honest. I need some motivation for being your everythang."

"What type of motivation you looking for? Monetary?" I asked, knowing the gold-digging type of style Ceazia put out.

"Money talks and bullshit walks," she quickly responded. "But since you're a real baller, I got every confidence you gon' pay what my shit weighs. And just so you'll know, my shit is heavier than a muthafucka."

"Oh yeah? Well, my money is long since we're talking American dollars here. And you're right about one thing, C."

"What's that, baby?" she purred.

"I *am* a real one, and don't you forget it."

"I won't. So, tell me how we gon' do this," Ceazia inquired.

"Well, how about this: you give me the 411 on my brother's murder, and I'll pay you tremendously for it."

"What makes you think I've got information?" Ceazia asked, playing her game well.

"C'mon, C. You know I must've figured the cops were hot on you for something. Even though you didn't kill Vegas an' nem, I know you got some word on who did it, right?"

Ceazia paused. "Well, I got some idea, but like I said, I ain't blabbing for free. Telling you the least little thing puts my life at risk."

"Nah, sexy. See, that's where you're wrong. Just let me cover you. You don't have to worry about trouble following you, and that's *my* word."

Considering I was about to blast Ceazia from this world made my word to her the truth. I ain't ever been dead before, but from what I believe, niggas are worry-free on the other side. My brother made a lot of mistakes, but he didn't deserve to die at the hands of Ceazia the way he did. Now this money-hungry bitch was too stupid to know that her life was in my hands. I listened to her game a little while longer.

"That's a deal. But that's going to cost you at least a hundred grand. Even though you say you will cover me, I need to get the fuck out of here. I need some lead-way in covering my own head after letting out that type of information."

"Not a problem. Any amount of money is worth it when it comes to my brother." I readily agreed, knowing that she would never live to get the loot anyway.

"Okay, baby, just let me know when and where," Ceazia said, agreeing to my proposition.

That was all I needed. I was glad Ceazia never stopped her gold-digging ways, because she was making things way too easy for me. I didn't know what terrific lie her shiesty ass had in her mind, but I was curious to hear it. She said she believed I was a true gamer, but her dumb ass never figured I might consider her info to be fake. Why would a hustler like me just give Ceazia a hundred grand going just on her word? Stupidity was about to lead her into an early grave, but not soon enough for me.

I smiled as my adrenaline began to flow at the thought of carrying out my mission. I knew within a matter of minutes, my penis would be wet and my plan complete. It was a beautiful thought.

CHAPTER 26

CAN'T TURN A HO INTO A HOUSEWIFE

MARRIED TO THE GAME

UNKNOWN MAN

Many niggas have said you can't turn a ho into a housewife, but no matter what, that is a statement I refused to believe when it came to Ceazia. I was doing all I could to turn her into that top-notch, untouchable housewife chick she used to be. And believe it or not, at times she even had me thinking she was almost there. Just earlier today we had lunch, and she was coming at me like she was ready to give up on this lifestyle as long as I was willing to hold her down. Of course I agreed to that.

Although she told me everything I wanted to hear, I still had to be on my shit. I told her I wasn't for no games, and if I saw any shit I didn't like, I was gon' fuck her up. I would hate to do it, but she had pushed me to that point. And she knew it, too. She could see the fire in my eyes when I warned her.

It was times like these when reality pistol-whipped me in the face. Ceazia didn't even know I'd been sitting in the cut watching her every move tonight. I made it a point to follow C and constantly check up on her every move, to see where her head was really at. And tonight I saw that bitch was back to basics. It looked like she was trying to fuck Snake again. And from the looks of things, she had him and his li'l soldier on some beef shit. I tell you, that bitch's pussy was deadly. It was like crack, and she had all us niggas running behind her like she held the last dime-piece in the city.

But I'd gotten hip to her game. Although when it came to her I could often be labeled as a "vick," I wasn't no damn fool. I knew when a bitch was down and doing bad, she'd tell a nigga whatever he wanted to hear, just so that she could get a few bucks out of him. And that had been Ceazia's scheme since Vegas's death. But I was using that to my advantage. I was trying to show her that I was that nigga that would put her back on that level she wanted to be on. Right now she was just so fucked up, she couldn't even see it. She thought that nigga, Snake, and his li'l soldier, Duke, was the best she could get next to Vegas. If it wasn't for them, Ceazia would be mine, and would be that housewife I knew she could be. So, what does that mean? Only one muthafucking thing: Those niggas had to go!

CHAPTER 27

JUST WHAT THE DOCTOR ORDERED

CEAZIA

That hundred grand was going to put me right back on top. Thank goodness for the gold between my legs and the hustle I got along with it. I knew Snake could only holdout so long, anyway. I mean, who else was going to put it on him like me? Who else was going to fulfill his every fantasy? Who else was going to deep-throat his big black dick, take it in the ass, and then allow him to drench her in a golden shower? Yes, I'd let him do whatever he wanted to me. That nigga had it like that.

That's right, no one but me, Ceazia Devereaux could handle Snake like he needed to be handled in the bedroom. And that's exactly why he decided to come back to me. This time I promised not to let him go.

But first things first. I had to get my exboyfriend off my back. I'd been popping a whole lot of bullshit to him lately, just so I could get a little change out of him every now and then. But this nigga was starting to act like he was losing his mind.

It had been a while since we had a tight relationship, but he just wouldn't let go. I'll admit, I would hit him up with some sex for some loot every now and then, but now, I couldn't get his ass off my back. He thought he fucking owned me. He should have known better than to think he could keep up with me day to day, because I was too fast for that. I kept a close watch on my surroundings.

I'd seen my ex following me and shit. Now he was even threatening to kill my ass if I fucked him over. As if I had his ring on my finger or something. Even if he put a ring on my finger, it wouldn't mean anything. I loved living in and all around the game, but my ex just wasn't who I had in mind to keep me laced.

Now that I had Snake in the palm of my hand, I didn't need this nigga running up on the scene, fucking shit up. I called him to keep things in order.

"What up, C?" My ex answered on the first ring.

"Nothing, baby. Just checking in. I thought you might want to know that I'm going out tonight," I lied, so he wouldn't be checking up on me while I was out with Snake.

"Out where? With who, Ceazia? Don't be giving me half of the fucking story. You know I wanna know where you going," he stated, asking question after question.

I had to straighten my shit up quick and make things sound convincing. "I got a money scheme. I'm planning to hit Snake up for some money—like a hundred grand," I blabbed out.

That was pretty good thinking. I had to pat myself on the back for putting things to him that way. I knew talk of money would keep me in the clear, just in case my ex found out I was with Snake without me having told him. My statement got his attention.

"Oh yeah? And just how do you plan to do that? Snake ain't as dumb as he looks, Ceazia. Don't forget he's been in the game for a while, training li'l soldiers how to be street-smart just like him. What makes you think you can pull a fast scheme on him?" he asked.

"It's simple. I told him I have some info on his brother's death, and he's willing to pay me for it. Once he does, I'm going to give him some bullshit story and then buck," I said in a conniving tone.

"I don't know about all that, C. Sounds kinda dangerous if you ask me," he replied.

"No, it's cool. Snake really thinks I got some info that will help him find his brother's killer. You don't know Snake like I do. He wants this information bad, and he's going to pay up."

"Damn, I see your mind is made up."

"Yeah, but baby, just think about how cool things gon' be between us once I get my hands on this money. You've had my back, and now I can do something nice for you. Me and you can even bounce out of here when I'm done."

"A'ight, C. You drive a hard bargain, girl. I just want you to be careful. Call me when you're done. And don't let me find out shit is different, or you know what you got coming," he stated then hung up the phone in my ear.

This nigga was serious. I guess I'd played one too many games with his heart. Now he was on some real ill shit. And the scary thing about it was I believed he would do exactly what he said. He would kill us all. The trip part about him threatening me was the fact this nigga begged me on a regular basis to be on some wifey shit; but I refused. I just couldn't do it. My hustle was just too strong for that shit. My ex-boyfriend couldn't be all I needed him to be to me. I just needed

Snake to realize what he had in a down-ass chick like me, and then he'd be glad to be my everything. Snake—oh that nigga can definitely get my all! Little did he know all he had to do was say the word and I would turn my whole life around.

I ran through one guy after another looking for a replacement for Vegas, or just simply trying to survive. When I thought about it, I'd really stooped to some low levels. I should have never been fucking that nigga, Duke. After spending the day with Li'l Momma, I felt really fucked up. I mean, that li'l chick had always looked up to me. And not only did I fuck her man, but I even lied to her about Judah. And what reason did I have to do that? None at all. I did it out of straight hate, just because he wouldn't fuck me. I'd done all that dirt to BJ, but she was the only one that was still in my corner after I told her about me and Vegas.

I could have never shared the story of his murder with anyone else. I lost all my friends behind that shit, and I wasn't even proven guilty. The only person besides my parents that I knew had my back was BJ, and look at the shit I'd done to her. How fucked up can one bitch be? I'd always told myself there were no friends or feelings in the game, but somehow I'd ended up with a conscience. First I was seeing shit during sex, and now I was actually feeling guilty for being on my grind. I felt with the life I was living, like I'd just bought myself a one-way express ticket to hell!

Ding-dong . . . ding-dong . . . ding-dong!

I rushed to the door to see who the hell was constantly ringing my doorbell. I looked out the peephole and saw that it was Duke. He had an evil look on his face. I took a deep breath and slowly cracked the door open.

"Why the fuck you ain't answering your phone?" he yelled while pushing his way through the door.

Duke looked mean as hell as he stared into my eyes. I feared his intentions for suddenly showing up at my home. I didn't know what I could say to calm him down, but I responded as quickly as I could.

"I didn't hear my phone ring," I said, confused at his aggression.

I didn't know why he was so upset, and more importantly, I didn't know why he'd just popped up at my house. He, of all people, should have known that was a definite no-no.

"Bitch, I've been calling you since I left the club. Your freak ass probably was on the phone with Snake. Where the fuck your phone at?"

"I am not giving you my phone. You are seriously tripping, Duke." I looked at him like he was crazy then walked away.

I thought I'd move to put a safe distance between the two of us, but Duke was up on me before I could see him coming. I was at his mercy as he continued to rant.

"What the fuck you say?" Duke said while grabbing my throat.

I couldn't believe Duke actually had the nerve to grab me like that. My blood boiled as I held his wrist in an attempt to loosen his grip. My eyes began to bulge as I gasped for air. The more I struggled, the angrier I became.

Noticing that I was damn near dead, Duke made the mistake of letting me go. As soon as he freed me, I ran to my purse and pulled out my chrome nine-millimeter and pointed right at him.

"I'm sure we both know that I know how to use this. And I never miss my target," I said, ready to kill his ass if necessary.

Duke smiled, licked his lips, and then calmly proceeded toward me. I became nervous, noticing that he was unmoved by my threat. He was going to force me to do or die. I put a bullet in the chamber as he came closer. This was surely an indication that I was serious.

"What you gon' do, C? You gon' kill me? You gon' shoot me? Huh?" Duke stated with his chest on the barrel of my gun.

Without blinking, we both looked at each other eye-to-eye. The only movement was the rise and fall of Duke's chest from his rampant breathing. Neither of us showed any fear. This was it; Duke was definitely calling my bluff. I could respect his gangsta, and I knew that bluffing was something he was trained to do as a soldier, but he was also forcing me into making a sound decision.

I stepped back and lowered the gun. Duke exhaled and gave a small, victorious grin. That was the wrong thing to do to an angry bitch like me. I raised my nine and pressed it hard against his temple. I wanted to blow his brains out, but I remained calm as I let him know I wasn't the one to be played with.

"You know I'll do it. Please don't make me," I said in a stern whisper.

"So that neither of us gets hurt, I'm going to leave and give you some time to think about what you just did," Duke said softly.

He turned his back toward me as a sign there was no fear then grabbed his hat and walked out the door.

Whew!

I exhaled then sat on the bed with trembling hands.

A real bitch would have shot his ass, I thought as I came down off my adrenaline rush. I figured I just didn't have it in me anymore. One thing for sure, I wasn't ready to commit another murder. Good thing Duke made the right move by leaving. He was right. I could have gotten one of us hurt or killed.

What if he would've turned and pulled his gun on me? I knew he was strapped, but luck had the situation in place so that Duke decided to walk away. If he stepped to me like that again, I was just gonna have to kill him. Next time, I might not be so lucky.

CHAPTER 28

A WOMAN SCORNED

DUKE

Seemed like C had lost her fucking mind. After that stunt she pulled, she had my head real fucked up. I couldn't even drive. I only made it to the corner. I had to stop and take a smoke after that shit. I guess that bitch just might have been a killer after all. It takes a bold bitch to pull a gun out on a nigga like me. Everybody on the streets knew I wasn't no punk, so for Ceazia to try me like that made my mind flinch. Pulling out on a gamer in a normal scenario would mean somebody, if not all people involved, would end up dead.

I wasn't sure how to react when C pulled-out on me. I ain't ever had a bitch come at me like that. All sorts of shit ran through my mind. But regardless, I had to play it cool, just to let that bitch know I wasn't the one to be fucked with.

After dealing with a crazy bitch like C, she made me miss BJ. I'd been so wrapped up in Ceazia, I didn't even give a fuck when BJ left me that Dear John letter. But then I began to sorta miss my old girl. I decided to give her a shout.

"Yeah, Duke." BJ answered the phone as though I was bothering her.

"What up?" I asked.

"Nothing. I'm with my boyfriend."

"Boyfriend?" I responded, surprised that she even had the balls to say that shit to me.

"Yeah, my boyfriend. I am seriously involved now, and we are planning to move to Atlanta together. So, please do me a favor and forget my number."

"Aw, nah, you got the game all wrong, shortie. You gon' always be mine. I suggest you tell ol' boy that he needs to wrap his shit up and be outta there when I get there," I stated angrily.

"Nigga, please. You ain't got no pull here no more. Don't come around here trying to go for bad, because you gon' mess around and get served if you do. My man ain't having no shit!"

And just like that, BJ hung up in my ear. That was another shocker. I thought ol' girl would always love me. I was her first, and I felt I should be her last and her everything. First C got at me like a mad chick, and then I learned BJ wasn't the little girl I used to mess with no more.

Still sitting in my car, not far from Ceazia's crib, I continued to take constant pulls on my blunt, quickly turning it into a roach. Soon I began to feel much more relaxed. I popped in a CD and prepared to pull off.

Just when I thought I couldn't take anymore surprises, I saw Snake drive past. There was only one place he could be headed. I figured it may be interesting to see just what was about to go down. I sat in the cut and watched as he entered the gate to Ceazia's home. A few minutes later, she came out and hopped in her car. Snake pulled off, and she followed directly behind him. Then I fell in line behind her. I was sure to keep my distance as I followed because I knew Snake would constantly be in his rearview. Ceazia, on the other hand, wouldn't be on point as much.

I continued to follow them as they hopped on the interstate and headed toward the oceanfront. I

222

already knew where they were headed. Snake could only be taking her one place—his favorite hotel at the beach. I thought this nigga would be smarter than that.

I thought about my next move as I watched them park then head to the room. All sorts of things ran through my mind.

Should I call Danielle and blow his spot up? Nah, that would be a bitch move. Should I just run up in there and blow his spot up? Nah, that would be a psycho move. Or maybe I should just call him and act like there is some sort of emergency.

Every option that ran through my mind seemed whack. There was no real cool way to handle this shit. I continued to sit and contemplate. Time was ticking, and I had to do something, but I had no idea what. Hell, with nothing else to lose, I decided to call Danielle.

"What, Duke?" She answered the phone with a serious attitude.

"Damn, ma, somebody would think we ain't cool. What's all the attitude about?" I quizzed.

"It's about cheating-ass niggas that call themselves boyfriends and their lying-ass nephews. I know the game, nigga! Now what?" Danielle snapped.

I had no idea what Danielle was talking about, but for some reason, I felt like it had something to do with lying for Snake about the strip club.

"What's going on, Danielle? I swear I don't know what you ranting about, and I won't know unless you tell me. Talk to me, baby," I begged.

"Look, Duke, I've gone through Snake's shit, and I know he's fucking with that trifling bitch, Ceazia. And I know you know all about it because she was there when you got shot," she spat.

One thing I knew from running game was never, never admit guilt, no matter how the odds are stacked against you. So with that in mind, I proceeded.

"What you mean, Danielle? Where is all this coming from? You got shit twisted, baby girl," I stated to get more information out of her.

Once I got her to tell me all she knew, I could come up with something that kept me clear. On the real, I was kinda glad Snake had been busted, but I needed to make sure she kept me as an ally.

"Look, Duke, I know I don't have it twisted. I saw her number and address written on a piece of paper in Snake's handwriting, then I found a card that had a picture of her with the same numbers that were written on the paper. And I saw her at the hospital with Snake the day y'all got shot. Although I have a law degree, it really doesn't take a genius to put two and two together here, Duke. Now, you can either tell me the truth or we can end this conversation now!" she yelled.

Snake was truly caught. There was no way out for him. But there was for me, on the other hand.

"Sweetie, I've been giving you hints for the longest. I told you the night we were going to the strip club. I told you that you were too good for him. It's only so much a nigga can do without just coming out and telling you directly." I spat a convincing game.

"How could he do this to me, Duke?" Danielle began a hysterical cry. "Look at the time. It's three in the morning and he's not even home. He's probably at the hotel with that whore now. As a matter of fact, I'm going down there."

Click.

Danielle slammed the phone down in my ear. That went easier than I thought. Now all I had to do was just wait for Danielle to come and blow the spot up.

CHAPTER 29

FINAL STRAW

UNKNOWN MAN

C said she was meeting up with Snake on some scheming shit. Knowing that chick couldn't be trusted, I took it upon myself to follow her. If she was going to be my girl, she was going to have to follow my rules. No more games!

It was like déjà vu as I sat outside the same hotel as before and looked through the crack of the curtain at Ceazia and Snake. I watched as C went into the bathroom and Snake sat on the bed playing with his gun nervously. I could see the suitcase sitting in the corner. I was assuming that was C's hundred grand. Maybe she wasn't lying this one time.

After ten minutes had passed, Ceazia came out of the bathroom draped only in a towel. As soon as she got within arm's reach, Snake grabbed her and pulled her on the bed. Although they were no longer completely in sight, I could tell some sort of sexual act was going on. I didn't know if this was part of her plan to buck or what, but I wasn't feeling that shit at all. Ceazia just had to try my patience. Now she was going to end up getting a nigga killed and herself hurt. Some bitches just don't get it. I saw I was going to have to bang her head in a few times to knock some sense into her ass. I never had the need to beat a chick, but now I saw why niggas did it.

I took the safety off my gun, cocked it back, putting one in the head, and headed for their room.

CHAPTER 30

RESTING DAY

SNAKE

This is it, I thought as I opened the hotel room door to let C in. I set the suitcase in the corner and sat on the bed. I ran scenario after scenario through my head as I waited for Ceazia to finish showering.

I should just go in there and put one in her head right now. Nah, too messy.

That thought went as soon as it came. I sat on the bed gun in hand, trying to decide what move to make. I guess the little bitch must've been anxious to hook up with me, because before I could think of another option, the shower turned off. I had to stick the gun under the mattress because Ceazia was headed out of the bathroom, draped in only a towel, and still dripping from head to toe.

C pranced over to me and let her towel drop to the floor. Although I was there to do her in, my dick still rose to the occasion, and C quickly noticed.

"Oh, it looks like someone misses me," she said.

I didn't respond. I just gave her a slight smile. C continued to touch and tease and caress me in the most seductive ways. Suddenly, my body told me how much I really needed her touch at that moment. I took advantage of the situation as she undressed me.

I threw C's wet body on the bed and dove into her already moistened kitten, ready to kill it first. Ceazia screamed out in pain as I drove every inch of my manhood inside her. I covered her face with the pillow as she pierced my back with her nails. The more she flinched with pain, the harder I fucked her and forced the pillow in her face to muffle her screams. Suddenly, I had thoughts of suffocating her, so I forcefully pressed the pillow in her face to the point where she physically began to struggle for air.

Ceazia dug and clawed my arms and back, but I maintained my focus. Like a crazed man, I never quit pounding her pussy as I continued to smother her. I was extremely turned on, thinking of her dying this way.

A loud noise interrupted my torturous sex just as I was about to reach my climax. We both jumped up, startled by the loud noise. We turned around to see the room door kicked in, and a figure standing before us with a gun aimed.

"What the fuck is going on? Bitch, you trying to play me? I told you what you had coming if you fucked me over!" he yelled, full of fury.

"Oh, thank God you're here, Bear. The money is in that suitcase in the corner. He was trying to rape me. I was screaming for help," Ceazia lied as she rushed to put her clothes on.

I couldn't believe this chick. She was putting on an act as though she was auditioning for an Oscar. And the fact that this punk-ass nigga bought it made it even worse. I sat baffled, not knowing what to say or do as I watched this performance before me.

"Get the fuck up, Snake," he demanded.

I stood to my feet slowly while scanning the room for a possible escape. He pressed the cold barrel of his Glock into my back.

I took a deep breath, realizing this may be the end. There was no need for negotiating. This nigga came here exactly for this. I thought I had gotten C, but it looked like she'd gotten me. That bitch was shiestier than I thought. I didn't know she had enough sense to even attempt to set me up. I guess the saying is true: What goes around comes around. Ceazia and my brother, Vegas, hit Bear for a hundred grand, and now the tables had turned. How funny is that? Now Bear and Ceazia were hitting me up for the exact same amount.

"You set me up, C? I shoulda just killed your ass while you were in the shower like I started to do. You think you're gonna get away with this, bitch?" I threatened.

"Shut the fuck up, punk. Ain't nobody set yo' bitch ass up. I have been after you for a while. I've been watching C and you for a while now. I could have done you in at the Coliseum, but that was too easy. I wanted to see you suffer. You and your brother have done enough. Now it's my turn to reign," that little pussy-ass nigga stated.

I was not only mad that my plan was blown, but I was even more upset that this pussy, Bear, had me at gunpoint.

"C, grab the money. I'm gon' do this nigga then you're coming home with me," he instructed.

Ceazia quickly jumped up and did exactly what he said. I watched her grab my bag. I knew my time had run out. I closed my eyes and reflected back on my life then said a silent prayer.

Bang!

My prayer was interrupted by a gunshot. I jumped to the floor and grabbed my gun once I realized I wasn't hit. I looked up to see Duke in the door and Bear slouched in the chair. This was one time I was extremely glad to see my little soldier.

Duke had put one into Bear's chest. Bear lay in the chair, bleeding from his mouth. Ceazia stood in the corner, motionless, and Duke stared at both of us. No one spoke a word, but if I had to guess, Ceazia knew for sure her time had run out. I knew I'd come here for one reason, and I wasn't leaving until it was done. So as planned, I aimed my gun to complete my mission.

"Get the fuck on the floor, C," I said, gun pointed directly at her.

"Please, Snake. I . . . I . . . I didn't know Bear was coming here. He's been stalking me and shit, and I know he's crazy, so I was just scared when I told him you tried to rape me. I know I shoulda told you about him stalking me, but I thought I had put a stop to him doing that."

"Yeah, bitch, so you put my life on the line instead of yours, right?"

Ceazia remained silent for a moment then she spoke up. "Snake, I was scared. Don't you want to know who killed Vegas? I thought that's what we were here for. Keep the money, just let me go," Ceazia pleaded, throwing the bag in my direction.

"Nah, bitch. I came to get my dick wet and to kill yo' ass. I've been knowing for a long time now that you were guilty. I was just waiting on the right moment to send you to see your maker."

"Please, Snake. That's some bullshit. Who told you I'm guilty? You know you can't be listening to what people on the streets say. I loved Vegas. I didn't kill him, and you don't have to kill me," Ceazia said, scheming.

"You're good, but not that damn good. And I don't believe that fake-ass story about how Bear got here, either. Your time was up whether that pussy-ass nigga showed up or not. Get the fuck on the floor like I told you, trick!"

Duke didn't hold his silence any longer. I was surprised to finally hear him speak up.

"Nah, nigga. You get on the ground," Duke said, gun pointing at me.

Again, I stood in the midst of confusion. I wasn't sure where this li'l nigga's head was anymore, but I didn't think he had the balls to really do me in, so I ignored him.

"How you gon' pull out on me, Li'l Soldier? Fuck you, Duke. C, get the fuck on the floor!" I repeated.

Bang!

Another shot rang out. This time I was hit. The pain was excruciating, like no other pain I'd ever felt before. I could feel my knees give out then I began to fall in what seemed like slow motion.

Bang! Bang!

I shot back as I fell to the floor. I felt paralyzed. My body became cold as I looked over at Duke lying near me. He huffed and puffed as he tried strenuously to catch a breath.

"How you gon' shoot me, Unc?" He forced out the words then exhaled his final breath.

That's when I looked over at Bear, who was still alive. Duke had not shot me. It was Bear. I'd shot my li'l soldier. Although I couldn't feel my body, my heart ached at Duke's death. I'd killed my nephew. I was hurting over the thought that my brother was gone, and now my li'l soldier was at peace. That was it. I refused to fight any longer. I was ready to die. What more did I have to live for? I lay silently and closed my eyes, preparing for eternal rest.

CHAPTER 31

QUICK GETAWAY

CEAZIA

In a crazy frenzy, I walked over to Snake and put my hand around his hand, grabbing his gun. I fired one final shot to make certain he wouldn't live. I stepped over his body and took a look at Duke. There was no need in wasting a bullet on him. Poor Duke didn't even have a fighting chance after Snake's shot hit him.

I looked over at Bear, who was struggling to speak. I stood over him silently, watching the blood trickling down his chin as he gripped his chest. The more he tried to talk, the more it pained me to see him struggle that way. I thought about how much control over my life Bear had lately, then I took him out of his misery.

Bang!

I put a final shot to Bear's head. I needed to be free from his grip, and this was the perfect opportunity. Besides, it was never in my plans to share any of the loot with Bear anyway. I grabbed the suitcase that held my money, picked up the rest of my belongings, and rushed out of the room, making sure to leave no traces. There was no way I could be involved with another murder. Couldn't do it!

I didn't even bother to run through their pockets or take any jewelry. I just fled as quickly as possible. I rushed to my car and hopped in. I sped out of the parking lot so fast I nearly ran into someone head on.

Beeep! Beeeep!

CHUNICHI

The crazy bitch laid on the horn. I looked up as I swerved around her.

"Oh shit!" I said aloud as I locked eyes with Snake's girlfriend, Danielle.

What the fuck is she doing here? I thought as I contemplated killing her too. I didn't have enough time. I could already hear the sirens in the distance. The police were on their way, and I needed to be no place in sight.

I sped home and grabbed my dog, Prissy, grabbed all my money, filled up a few bags of clothes, and hit the road, leaving all else behind. I had to get the fuck out of dodge. And this time, I was going far, far away. Catch me if you can!

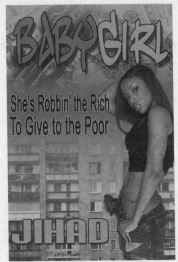

OCTOBER 2005
1-893196-23-2

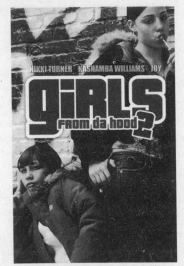

OCTOBER 2005
1-893196-28-3

NOVEMBER 2005
1-893196-25-9

DECEMBER 2005
0-9747025-9-5

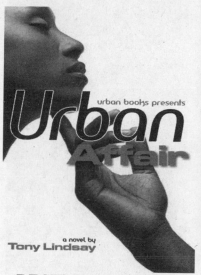

DECEMBER 2005
1-893196-27-5

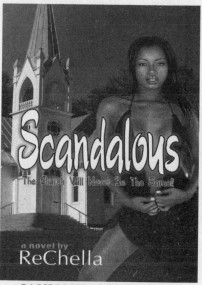

JANUARY 2006
1893196-30-5

JANUARY 2006
1893196-29-1

FEBRUARY 2006
1-893196-41-0

URBAN BOOKS PRESENTS

PAY'BACK

a street saga by
roy glenn

FEBRUARY 2006
1-893196-37-2

I Don't Wanna be RIGHT

ALISHA YVONNE
AUTHOR OF LOVIN' YOU IS WRONG

MARCH 2006
1-893196-32-1

URBAN BOOKS
PRESENTS

GIGOLO'S
get lonely too

MARCH 2006
1-893196-33-X

URBAN BOOKS
PRESENTS

Make You Love Me

LA TONYA Y. WILLIAMS

APRIL 2006
1-893196-34-8

OTHER URBAN BOOKS TITLES

Title	Author	Quantity	Cost
Drama Queen	LaJill Hunt		$14.95
No More Drama	LaJill Hunt		$14.95
Shoulda Woulda Coulda	LaJill Hunt		$14.95
Is It A Crime	Roy Glenn		$14.95
MOB	Roy Glenn		$14.95
Drug Related	Roy Glenn		$14.95
Lovin' You Is Wrong	Alisha Yvonne		$14.95
Bulletproof Soul	Michelle Buckley		$14.95
You Wrong For That	Toschia		$14.95
A Gangster's girl	Chunichi		$14.95
Married To The Game	Chunichi		$14.95
Sex In The Hood	White Chocalate		$14.95
Little Black Girl Lost	Keith Lee Johnson		$14.95
Sister Girls	Angel M. Hunter		$14.95
Driven	KaShamba Williams		$14.95
Street Life	Jihad		$14.95
Baby Girl	Jihad		$14.95
A Thug's Life	Thomas Long		$14.95
Cash Rules	Thomas Long		$14.95
The Womanizers	Dwayne S. Joseph		$14.95
Never Say Never	Dwayne S. Joseph		$14.95
She's Got Issues	Stephanie Johnson		$14.95
Rockin' Robin	Stephanie Johnson		$14.95
Sins Of The Father	Felicia Madlock		$14.95
Back On The Block	Felicia Madlock		$14.95
Chasin' It	Tony Lindsey		$14.95
Street Possession	Tony Lindsey		$14.95
Around The Way Girls	LaJill Hunt		$14.95
Around The Way Girls 2	LaJill Hunt		$14.95

Girls From Da Hood	Nikki Turner		$14.95
Girls from Da Hood 2	Nikki Turner		$14.95
Dirty Money	Ashley JaQuavis		$14.95
Mixed Messages	LaTonya Y. Williams		$14.95
Don't Hate The Player	Brandie		$14.95
Payback	Roy Glenn		$14.95
Scandalous	ReChella		$14.95
Urban Affair	Tony Lindsey		$14.95
Harlem Confidential	Cole Riley		$14.95

Urban Books
74 Andrews Ave.
Wheatley Heights, NY 11798

Subtotal: _____

Postage:_____ Calculate postage and handling as follows: Add $2.50 for the first item and $1.25 for each additional item

Total: _____

Name: _____

Address:_____

City: _____ State: _____ Zip: _____

Telephone: (   ) _____

Type of Payment (Check: ___   Money Order: ___)

All orders must be prepaid by check or money order drawn on an American bank.

Books may sometimes be out of stock. In that instance, please select your alternate choices below.

Alternate Choices:

1._____

2._____

PLEASE ALLOW 4-6 WEEKS FOR SHIPPING